# In Your Dreams

Colin Neenan

# In Your

# Dreams

HARCOURT

BRACE

& COMPANY

San Diego

New York

London

Requests for permission to make copies
of any part of the work should be mailed to:
Permissions Department, Harcourt Brace & Company,
6277 Sea Harbor Drive, Orlando, Florida 32887-6777.

Library of Congress Cataloging-in-Publication Data
Neenan, Colin, 1958–
In your dreams/by Colin Neenan.—1st ed.
p.    cm.
Summary: Fifteen-year-old Hale's life becomes very complicated
when he helps his older brother woo the girl he
is secretly in love with himself.
ISBN 0-15-200885-3 ISBN 0-15-200884-5 (pbk.)
[1. Interpersonal relations—Fiction.   2. Self-confidence—Fiction.
3. Brothers—Fiction.]   I. Title.
PZ7.N383In   1995
[Fic]—dc20        94-31058

The text was set in Perpetua.
Designed by Trina Stahl
First edition
A B C D E
A B C D E (pbk.)

Printed in Hong Kong

*To Julia*

*. . . and so I follow with my eyes*

*Where some boy, with a girl upon his arm,*

*Passes a patch of silver . . . and I feel*

*Somehow, I wish I had a woman, too,*

*Walking with little steps under the moon,*

*And holding my arm so, and smiling.*

*Then I dream—*

—Edmond Rostand
*Cyrano de Bergerac*

# Chapter 1

1 saw her first. I was sitting under the big beach umbrella, trying to avoid skin cancer, when she unfurled her towel and shimmied out of her shorts like she was taking off her clothes. Even with the bikini bottom on, if she'd shimmied out of her shorts like that at school, say in a crowded hallway between classes—lockers slamming, jerks pushing everybody else around— if she'd shimmied like that at school, she'd have been arrested.

But at the beach it happens all the time; no one even notices, supposedly, which is crazy. I noticed. My older brother, Tom, and his friend

Willy noticed. And Dad noticed, too, even though Matilda, my stepmother, sap that she is, never suspected a thing.

Women, girls, females—they're all insanely gullible. It doesn't matter if they're smart. It's like God or somebody else who wanted the species to survive snipped a piece out of the female brain that makes them psychopathically gullible. Otherwise they'd never associate with us. They'd know it's no joke—we really *do* want to have sex with every one of them, give or take a few.

I tried to explain this to my just recently pubescent younger sister. (When she was making up the shopping list at breakfast three weeks ago, Matilda asked Tracy if she needed Tampax; Matilda is pathetically open-minded about discussing menstruation and masturbation and just about anything else you'd just as soon not hear about.) Anyway, I tried to tell Tracy the scoop about boys and sex and her boyfriend, Mickey, but she didn't listen; she looked at the black nail polish on her nails like she was deaf.

It's genetic. Girls don't want to hear it. Even if you're worried about them getting hurt, even if you're actually just trying to be nice, they don't want to hear it. And when they do hear it, they don't listen.

The girl with the bathing suit had long, thin legs, and even the backs of her knees were tanned and pretty. It was about the first thing I noticed. I know how romance works—I know the first thing you're *supposed* to notice is her eyes, or her *smile,* or the way she jumps rope, but she had her back to me and the first thing I saw was the backs of her knees.

She sat down on her blanket and—very carefully, so as to avoid besmirching herself with sand—rubbed in one of those glistening tanning oils. I watched her hands running up her arms, down her legs, up her legs. Tom kept trying not to watch. Willy was wearing his dark shades and had his head twisted halfway between her and the ocean so you couldn't be sure what he was looking at unless you knew him. She popped the top back onto her tanning-oil bottle and rolled over and lay on her stomach. I looked at her legs, at the small of her back, at her thin arm connected to her shoulder. Then I looked at her face, her cheek against the blanket, her eyes open, watching me. *Damn.*

I pulled my eyes away, stared at my knees. Girls hate it when guys watch their bodies, and they really hate it when *ugly* guys watch their bodies. They wear tight jeans and tank tops and bathing suits, but they just want to know in a theoretical sort of way that guys look at them. If you admit to them you've been looking at the curve in the small of their back, they'll hate you for it.

I should've gone back to the house for my sunglasses. What a moron. Out of the corner of my eye I tried to steal a small, passing glance, but she was still looking my way. She was watching me, and I thought I saw a little twist of a smile. Not a friendly smile, not the inviting kind of smile girls give Willy and even sometimes Tom (although he never notices). This was not a girl-smiling-at-a-guy smile. This smile was more like the way my sister looks at me when I tell Matilda that, of course, the party I'm going to will be supervised; of course, there won't be any beer; of course, I'll thank Mr. and Mrs. Whoever. This smile knew what was going on. This smile knew I had burned into permanent memory the shape of the small of her back. I stared at my knees and sighed.

"What is it about the shine of tanning oil that's sexy?" Willy asked, like he was talking to himself. I knew it was a real question—he honestly didn't know why tanning oil made a girl look sexy, and he thought it was kind of weird, now that he'd stopped to think about it.

This happened to Willy a lot: Can running water get colder than thirty-two degrees Fahrenheit? Why can't we eat wood? Why does it feel so good to get a hickey? Tom told me that once in the fourth quarter of a game when they were down by five, Willy ran back into the huddle after talking to the coach during a time-out, and he turned and asked Tom if he knew where wind came from. "Shouldn't all the wind in the world die down, eventually?" he'd asked, mostly to himself.

Now it was the shine of tanning oil on a girl's body. And he was just thinking out loud—talking—like she didn't have ears. "This is nutty," Willy said, at the top of his lungs. "Why are shiny bodies more attractive?" He was even louder than before.

"How should I know?" Tom asked, embarrassed, exasperated. Tom got embarrassed asking for extra ketchup at McDonald's, so it was kind of weird, him and Willy being friends when Willy would sing "Hark the Herald Angels Sing" in the boys' room and not be embarrassed. "Hey, it's my favorite song," he'd say, and shrug.

I looked back over. Her eyes were closed—she looked like she was sleeping—and I just stared. She had blond hair pulled back into a bushy ponytail, high cheekbones, and a mouth too wide for her face. She wasn't knock-you-down pretty, which as far as I was concerned made her more attractive. I was staring at her lips when her eyes bounced open. Son of a bitch! I grabbed my T-shirt, got out of my beach chair, and walked out into the sun, toward the boardwalk. Ordinarily, I would've waited for the next cloud to drift by because the direct sunlight on my sunburn felt like an electric range had wrapped its coils around my shoulders, but it's hard sometimes to sit around waiting for a cloud.

"Hale?" Dad called, but I didn't want to go back, so I pretended not to hear. Why couldn't she have just been asleep? But then I thought, Why do I like the idea so much of watching girls when they're asleep? Am I a sexual deviant? A sleepomaniac? I stared down at the hot, bright sand. It seemed like I spent a good part of my life wondering if I was a sexual deviant.

Up at the boardwalk, I walked straight across into the arcade. The same four kids as yesterday were in the back, playing Skee Ball; the same Vietnam-vet-looking guy was playing pinball.

What did he think about, standing there for hours playing pinball? What did he dream about? What miracle did he hope was going to change his life? I watched him play, feeling the tight, sunburned skin on my shoulders cool off in the shade.

I always got burned. One of my earliest memories is of me and Tracy standing in the kitchen of some beach house arguing about whose shoulders were more sunburned. Every year our family has gone to the beach for a week—first with Mom, now with Matilda—every year I bring SPF-25 sunscreen, every year Dad rents a big beach umbrella, and every year I get tired of sitting in the shade and go out and play Frisbee or catch in the water for five or ten minutes and end up getting scorched.

I was no good with pain. Some people didn't seem to mind. Tom jogged and ran wind sprints all summer long to be in shape for football season, and he'd push himself so hard sometimes he'd puke. Me, I couldn't do that to myself. The closest I got was occasionally doing math homework.

I stood in the arcade, putting my hand gently on my shoulder, which felt like it was cooking on low. How does it work with sunburn, anyway? Does the skin actually suck up the heat? I shook my head; I was starting to sound like Willy.

I looked out at the ships on the horizon. They never seemed to move. You could watch them all day long, and they never seemed to budge until they disappeared altogether. Some girls walked by on the boardwalk, but I kept watching the ships. Sometimes I wondered if it'd be healthier to just not look at girls at all, to go live in a monastery. It was probably too late now, though, because I already had all these memories of smalls of backs and thighs and bikinis, and the memories would probably never go away, and I'd just commit suicide because I was in a monastery and would never see tanning-oiled skin again.

Suddenly something caught my eye down on the beach: Willy was standing up and walking over to the girl in the bathing suit. I could see his lips move even from the boardwalk, and my heart sank into my stomach. Instinctively, I lurched forward, wanting to help, wanting to run out and wave my hands over my head. *No! No! Don't do it, don't talk to him, he's dangerous!* I stood there feeling like I was watching someone drown. What could I do? Walk down there and tell her about Lisa, Willy's girlfriend back home? Tell her about the girl Tuesday night? The one Willy met on the boardwalk. (He'd won a little stuffed dragon throwing baseballs and just handed it to her and introduced himself. We didn't see him again until the "Today" show.)

The girl in the bathing suit laughed at something Willy said. It was hopeless now. Willy had her. He was like a whirlpool with girls, and this girl was already spinning round and round. And so what? What did I care? I didn't even know this girl.

I turned and walked through the arcade and on across to Main Street. The house we were renting was four blocks up and over on Piper, but Main Street had boutiques and restaurants with awnings to duck under along the way. I dodged from awning to awning like it was raining.

What if I went back to the beach and paid a little kid to hand the girl in the bathing suit a note? *The guy you're talking to is nice, but he's already got a girlfriend. Her name's Lisa. She bakes him cookies. Sincerely, A Stranger.*

It would only cost a buck or two to get some seven-year-old kid to walk over and hand it to her. Plus, even if she tried pumping the kid about who I was, what would a seven-year-old remember? *Some guy; I don't know.* We all look alike to a seven-year-old.

I took a left on Piper, squinting in the sunshine.

The only problem with the note idea was, How many people on the beach could know Willy had a girlfriend named Lisa? The girl in the bathing suit would know right away it was me, the ugly guy with the sunburn she caught looking at her. Maybe she wouldn't even believe it. Maybe she'd think I was just being jealous.

A half-block from the house I could hear Tracy's music. She listens to this juvenile-delinquent stuff about rape and incest and motorcycles and lots of stuff I wouldn't have let my daughter listen to, but Matilda said it was a matter of respect, letting people listen to what they like. Dad just sat there whenever we talked about Tracy's music. He sat and stared at the sugar bowl and chewed his toothpicks. (He'd quit smoking sixteen years ago but still popped toothpicks into his mouth when he was worried.) You could tell he hated thinking about Tracy listening to this stuff, hated thinking about Tracy believing the stuff in those songs was what life was really like, but he never said anything.

Inside, Tracy was sitting on a couch, reading a book, her boom box screaming next to her, the fan on the coffee table blowing her hair around like she was in a snowstorm. Tracy had dyed black hair and wore black T-shirts with the sleeves torn off. She'd talk to Tom sometimes, but somehow she knew it was me opening the screen door and didn't even look up from her book—another dice-'em-up horror story. All she did was read, listen to music, and play her guitar. She hadn't been out in the daylight since we'd arrived.

"Nice tan!" I hollered over the music, but she just turned a page like I was dust on a table. I got a Coke out of the refrigerator and went into the room I shared with Tom and Willy and shut the door. I sat down at the foot of my bed and wondered when Willy first had sex. He and Tom were going to be seniors—two years older than me. How many times had Willy had sex by the time he was my age? I knew he'd had sex last fall with Cindy White in the backseat of his parents' Buick because Cindy went around bragging about it. I wondered how many other girls Willy'd had sex with, and then I started wondering if Tom had ever had sex with a girl. And then I started worrying about Tracy. And the girl on the beach. She smiled like she knew what was going on, but girls never *really* know what's going on. Would she do stuff with Willy even though he had a girlfriend? She didn't look like the type, but types could change around guys like Willy.

I lay back on the bed and followed the cracks

in the ceiling. They looked like economic indicators, going up a little, then down a lot. Willy only had that night. We were leaving early in the morning to go home. Could he get this girl to fall in love with him overnight? Would she just forget to ask him if he had a girlfriend back home? How did that work? I couldn't picture Willy lying about it, but maybe she wouldn't care. Maybe when a girl met someone like Willy, she forgot on purpose to ask about girlfriends back home.

I closed my eyes. My mind started dropping back through the mattress like I was falling asleep. I could handcuff him. But to what? One of those wire trash cans they have down at the beach? That wouldn't be enough. He'd dump out the garbage, carry the thing down to the water to wash away the smell, and then invite the girl in the bathing suit to a midnight picnic on the sand. And she'd feel sorry for him because some jerk had handcuffed him to a trash can. She'd never ask about girlfriends back home then. You'd never even think that a guy handcuffed to a garbage can would have a girlfriend back home. You see a guy handcuffed to a garbage can and you just wonder how he gets around. Does he have a driver's license? What happens when he rolls over in his sleep? Does he shampoo his hair with one hand?

"Hey. Hey, buddy."

"Huh?" I woke up with a start—even though I wasn't really asleep—and saw Willy. "What? What?" I asked, worried, like I was late, like I'd missed something—a game, an exam. Then I remembered because it was daylight and I could see the bedroom and Willy and Tom in swim trunks—I remembered we were at the beach.

"Guess what?" Willy was smiling.

"What?" I asked, hopeless, remembering it all now—the beach and the girl in the bathing suit with the legs and the eyes and the smile and Willy talking to her.

"Guess who has a date tonight."

"You do," I said, already resigned to it, but Willy shook his head.

"*We* do."

# Chapter 2

**Y**ou guys are on drugs," I said, climbing out of bed. "Forget it."

Tom and Willy stood between the beds, blocking my way.

"Sheri wants you to come," Willy said. "I swear to God."

"What. As a mascot? No way!" I didn't get my hopes up easily, and when they woke me up and Willy said *we* had a date, I knew instantaneously he didn't mean *we* the way most people would define *we*. It turned out *we* meant that Sheri—Sheri was the girl on the beach with the legs and the eyes and the smile—that Sheri had said she and her friend Trish would play miniature golf with Tom and Willy as long as they dragged me along.

"They want a chaperone," Tom explained, sounding like he couldn't believe I wasn't being more reasonable.

"Tell them to call a chaperone service. I'm out. Forget it."

"Oh, come on, Haley," Tom said, desperate. *Haley.* That was rich. All of a sudden I was cute little brother Haley again.

"Sheri said you have an honest face," Willy said.

I turned away, waving my hands in front of me like I didn't want my picture taken. "Forget it! Just forget it!"

"Haley. She likes you."

It wasn't funny anymore. I stepped up onto Tom's bed and walked across it to the door. They'd closed the door behind them when they came in, and now Tom jumped in front of it before I could get it open.

"She really likes you. I mean it."

"Give me a break, will you?" The kidding was over. "Just leave me alone."

"I don't mean like that," Tom said. "I mean she asked about you. She wanted to know your name."

"It's Hale. You want me to spell it for you?"

"Oh, come on, Haley," Tom begged. "Please? I'm asking please."

I stood there. I looked at my watch.

Five hours later to the minute, Sam's Miniature Golf loomed in front of us, and Tom kept pushing his hair back off his forehead. He was pretty good-looking but he didn't know it, which doesn't help when you're a guy. But even if he'd realized what he looked like, he still would've been nothing compared to Willy. Willy was six-foot-two with curly hair and looked like he could throw touchdown passes in his sleep. I glanced over at the two of them and realized that if I were Tom, I'd find a different friend.

"Sheri and Trish," Tom said out loud, making sure he had the names right. Tom was the nervous type; he worried about exams and homework and always studied hard. Now he stared down at the slats in the boardwalk like he was walking onto the field for the big game. "Sheri and Trish," he said again.

I watched him out of the corner of my eye, then looked at Willy. They wanted a chaperone; they were going to get a chaperone. They'd be lucky if they held hands with these girls by the time I was through.

"Where do these girls come from, anyway?" I asked, but no one said anything. Willy just smiled and looked over at Tom, and then Tom smiled. "What's so funny?"

"Should we tell him?" Willy asked.

"What. Are they from Kansas?"

Willy twisted his face into a foot-long grin. "Bascom."

"What?" I looked at Tom. "Are you serious?"

"We didn't find out until we were leaving," Tom said.

"They thought Tom had a Pennsylvanian accent."

"I didn't even know there *was* a Pennsylvanian accent."

I just kept blinking, incredulous. "They're really from Bascom? You're really going to go out with Bascom girls?"

Bascom was the Beverly Hills of northern Virginia. In the summer you could drive around Bascom and never see a house because they were all three acres from the road and hidden by little private forests. The Bascom Salvation Army store looked like Bloomingdale's.

"You guys! What if someone finds out?"

Willy couldn't stop smiling. "Finds out what?"

"I don't believe this," I said, refusing to look at either one of them. Bascom wasn't just rich—it was Oakdale's football nemesis. For three years they had kept us out of the state play-offs. The year before, the game had been at Bascom, and three Oakdale kids got arrested for fighting, even though the cops couldn't say who they were fighting and no Bascom kids got in trouble. If we'd won, nobody would've cared, but we got clobbered 41–16 and the three arrests became this big, momentous *issue*. Even the *Washington Post* had articles about it. Then at the Oakdale-Bascom basketball game in January there was a small riot, and six kids and a cop went to the hospital. The second game was canceled.

I kept shaking my head. "Do they know who you are?"

Willy was still grinning. "Sheri couldn't believe we played for Oakdale and didn't drool."

"What a sense of humor."

Sam's had a big, blue neon sign with a guy holding a golf club over his shoulder, ready to swing away—which didn't make much sense because no one winds up to swing a golf club on a miniature golf course. I saw Sheri and Trish standing to the side of the entrance. Sheri looked different with clothes on. She was wearing her hair down on her shoulders and had on jeans and this oversized pink oxford shirt. She looked pretty, but nothing to give you epileptic seizures. It bugged me how my heart kept going on like I was meeting a movie star. Trish wore one of those shirts hanging off one shoulder and a tight denim skirt. She was shorter than Sheri and had mounds of curly black hair that made her face seem small. Just looking at the four of them smiling, saying hello, I wished I wasn't there.

"Thanks for coming," Sheri said, shaking my hand.

"Yeah, well . . ." I backed away and turned my face toward the ocean. Sheri wanted us all to play golf, but I said forget it and walked over and sat down on a bench by the first hole.

"What's the book?" Sheri asked, walking over after getting her ball and putter.

*"Whatever Doesn't Kill Me,"* I said, reading the title off the cover, feeling my hands sweat like this was some sort of college interview.

"What's it about?"

I kept my head tilted down like I was still reading. "Life. Death. Reality," I said. Sheri didn't say anything, and I looked up with my eyes without moving my head. She was just watching me.

"Boys against the girls," Trish called out. She had this cute, squeaky, "rich" voice that sounded like she'd spent her life practicing it in front of a mirror.

"Want to bet on the two football stars?" Sheri asked.

I talked to my book. "How 'bout a hundred-thousand dollars?"

"How 'bout fifty cents."

"Whatever you can afford," I said, turning a page.

I told myself I wouldn't look up, I wouldn't watch, but the first hole was right in front of me. Trish's shot ricocheted off the windmill and landed in the grass by a little cement pond, but then Sheri hit a hole in one and glanced my way before I had a chance to look back at my book.

"Double or nothing?"

"Sure," I said to my book, feeling my face burn, embarrassed. I tried to read but kept getting distracted and looking up to see where they were. I could hear Tom and Willy talking and Trish laughing her Minnie Mouse laugh, but Sheri hardly said a word.

At the eighteenth hole, the four of them looked like they were at a funeral. Tom was the last one to tee up, and Trish squeezed Sheri's arm as they both watched. Tom's shoulders and arms looked stiff, like they were made out of reinforced concrete. He took a swipe. I couldn't see the ball, so I followed Sheri's eyes. They got bigger and bigger and then deflated as Trish screamed. What happened? For half a second, I couldn't tell, but then I saw Tom just stand there and Trish jump all over Sheri like she was auditioning for a game show. They'd won.

Back out on the boardwalk, Trish told us that Sheri was one of the top five girl golfers in Virginia. Willy complained it was unfair having a ringer.

"Aaaawwwww," Trish said in mock sympathy, patting Willy's arm. I watched her hand linger on his arm and rolled my eyes, but Willy was so used to girls flirting with him, it was like he didn't even feel it. I gave Sheri the dollar without lifting my head up to look at her.

"It's been nice doing business with you," she said.

Trish wanted to get some beer and go back

to their room at the hotel, so Willy stopped in at a fancy sandwich place and used his fake ID to buy three six-packs. I was tired of chaperoning and wasn't in the mood to watch people get drunk and make out, so when Willy came back out with the beer, I waved to Trish and Sheri.

"Nice meeting you," I said.

"Where do you think *you're* going?" Sheri asked. It actually woke my heart up.

"What. I've got a dentist appointment."

"Fine. I'll go with you."

Trish threw her hands up. *"Sheri."*

"Hey. Either all five of us go back to the hotel, or I'm not going."

"Oh, come on."

"They're not creeps," I told her.

Sheri gave me a look like she was trying to tell me something. "Maybe they're not the ones I'm worried about."

Trish's mouth dropped open. *"Sheri."*

"I've got it!" Willy said. "Let's all go meet Hale's dentist."

"That's a good idea."

I looked at Willy. "Whose side are you on?"

We all walked back down the boardwalk toward their hotel—a white high-rise right on the boardwalk. The hotel lobby was covered with brass and mirrors. A guy with a mustache and a bow tie stood at the front desk. Trish and Sheri called out hello to Phil, and he smiled and winked.

The girls had come to the beach with Trish's parents, but they had their own room. Trish opened the door, and I went in and walked by the boom box on the dresser and some lacy underwear on the floor and out to the terrace overlooking the ocean. We were on the tenth floor, the penthouse, and down below was the beach and the water and the lights shining all the way up the boardwalk. No wonder people liked being rich. I left the terrace light off and walked over and sat down in a lounge chair. Trish came out to give me a beer, but I told her I didn't drink.

"Never? Are you, like, religious?"

"Yeah," I said. "Mm-hmm."

That scared her away pretty quick, and I sat there in the dark, looking out at the lights on the boats. I'd been drunk once in my life, at a party up in New York just before we moved away, so I knew that with enough beer anything seems possible. And that's not good. You can do incredibly stupid things when anything seems possible. Pathetically stupid.

"Does your brother always drink so fast?"

I jumped half a foot. Sheri stood just outside the sliding glass door.

"How many has he had?"

"Two? Three? I'm not sure. Trish says she wants to go swimming, but she always acts a little drunker than she really is."

Inside someone turned up the music. Light was shining out and hitting Sheri on the side of her face.

"Tom's all right," I said. "He's probably just a little nervous."

"Nervous about what?"

"You've never looked in a mirror?"

Sheri couldn't have seen me in the dark, but she turned in the direction of my voice. "Is there something about me you don't like?"

"What. No." I said it too fast, like I was trying to hide something.

Sheri smiled, or it looked like a smile on the half of her face I could see. "Do you want me to turn on the light?"

"No thanks."

"It's right here."

"That's OK."

"But you can't read your book."

"I'll live."

Sheri shook her head and laughed. My heart was racing like a maniac. "Well, come on inside at least. Trish wants us all to start dancing."

"Yeah. OK."

Sheri stepped inside. I breathed like I had the wind knocked out of me. She was just being friendly. Nice. Just nice, that's all. A nice person. People think it's amazing when pretty girls are nice. Of course they're nice. Everybody's nice to them; everybody smiles at them. Sheri was just being nice, coming out on the porch. Petting a mangy dog.

"Good doggie. Good doggie," I said, out loud. "Roll over. Play dead."

I sat back, crossed my arms, and looked out at the lights on the horizon. It wasn't quite real, sitting alone in the dark, faraway, untouchable, overlooking everything. I glanced down at the streetlights along the boardwalk.

Boardwalk and Park Place. I remembered back in New York, me and Jimmy and Kevin playing Monopoly. Kevin was a real wheeler-dealer who always won whenever you traded with him, so Jimmy and I always tried to work deals without him. The three of us used to hang out all the time in a McDonald's on Broadway and Eighty-second, but last summer Dad moved the family down to

Virginia to live with Matilda, and I hadn't seen Kevin or Jimmy since.

Trish tripped walking out onto the terrace. "We're going skinny-dripping," she announced, and then doubled over laughing as she walked back inside. "Did you hear that? Skinny-dripping!"

I stared out into the blackness. Had Willy really convinced Sheri to go skinny-dipping? He was incredible. He deserved a trophy. How did he do it? I shook my head and walked over to the sliding glass door to take a look inside.

Someone had draped a towel over the lamp shade, making the room dark like a bar. I was confused at first because things were mixed up. Willy and Trish were dancing by the dresser and staring at each other, and *Tom* was talking to Sheri. I'd been sure Willy was going to get Sheri; it just made sense. I never pictured *Tom* and Sheri.

They were sitting opposite each other on the sides of the two beds, both of them leaning forward as Tom rambled on and on about something he thought was hysterical. You could tell he was pretty drunk because he was smiling and throwing his hands around and tilting his head way back as he drank his beer. Tom couldn't even tell a joke right, but when he got drunk he thought he was a regular riot. He looked over his shoulder at Trish and Willy.

"So where can you go skinny-dipping around here?" Tom asked.

I looked for a big rock to crawl under. He was *dying* to go skinny-dipping, and it was so obvious, it was pathetic.

Trish flung her arm toward the terrace. "Did you see that thing out there? That ocean?" She laughed at her own joke and grabbed Willy's arm and pulled him toward the door.

Sheri stood up and waved for me to come in.

"I'm not going skinny-dipping," I said.

"No one's going skinny-dipping. Relax." Sheri closed the door behind us.

Outside we walked toward the end of the boardwalk, where the lights stopped like it was the edge of a cliff. On the steps down to the beach, I took off my flip-flops and let my feet sink through the cool sand to the warmer sand below. My eyes weren't used to the dark, but I could hear Tom opening another beer. I slowed down, trying to let everyone go on ahead, but Sheri and then Tom slowed down and walked along beside me. Trish skipped ahead singing, "We're off to see the wizard, the wonderful wizard of Oz. . . ." Willy followed her.

"Don't let her kill herself," Sheri called to Willy.

"Don't worry."

From somewhere out in the darkness, I could just barely hear Trish saying, "She acts like I'm mentally incompetent."

"You *are* mentally incompetent," Sheri muttered under her breath.

"Willy has that effect on girls," I said.

Sheri snorted. "What am I? Chopped liver?"

"No, it's just Trish got there first, that's all."

"You're telling me the only reason I didn't swoon over Willy is that Trish got there first?"

"I doubt you're exactly a swooner."

"But I would have fallen for him."

"Eventually."

"You don't know me very well."

"You don't know Willy very well."

"Hale-y," Tom said. Two different notes, the first high, the second low. "Hale-y. Quit giving her a hard time."

"What."

"He's just trying to get to you," Tom said.

"Wait a second," I said. "You don't think she's the type?"

"What type?"

"He's making it up! Just ignore him."

"Willy had you figured out like that," I said, snapping my fingers.

"Why? What'd he say?"

"Hale-y!" The first note high, the second note higher. "Hale-y! Knock it off!"

"He said you're the smart-pretty type who thinks she's got everybody figured out. And he said you're a lot more insecure than you let on."

"Willy said all that, huh?"

"Hale." Tom's voice was thicker, less focused, but I wasn't paying attention.

"He said what works for your type are flowers."

"Well, he's got *me* figured out."

"Hale," Tom said, quickly, like he was running out of breath. I didn't notice.

"Flowers, a sense of humor, and honesty. Those are the three key ingredients for your type. I mean, combined with curly-hair good looks."

"Do you really think honesty's that important?"

"Ha—," Tom started to say. Or at least that's what I thought he had started to say, until I realized he was throwing up.

# *Chapter 3*

*1* didn't know what to say. Tom had apologized two or three hundred times and walked down to the shore to clean himself up, and Sheri and I were alone. Together. On a dark beach. She couldn't even *see* me. It was like something I dreamed about, only in the dream I was ready for it.

"You have any brothers or sisters?" I asked, and wanted to slap myself. I was as bad as Tom.

"An older brother," Sheri said. "He's at school up in Boston."

"Oh." I stood there. What was wrong with me? This was my chance to *talk* to this girl, to say something that only she could ever understand. This was my chance to maybe not even say anything, to just *be* with this girl.

"You have a younger sister, don't you?" she asked.

"Sort of, yeah. She's more like a derelict, actually."

"A what?"

"My dad lets her get away with murder because she plays the guitar and listens to his music."

"What kind of music does he like?"

"Hmm?" I was looking for Tom. "Oh. No, I mean his own music. He writes music. Besides being an accountant." This wasn't what I wanted to talk about, but I had no idea what I *did* want to talk about. "I think a long time ago all Dad wanted to do was write music, but Mom got him to wake up and smell the starvation. That's one of her expressions—wake up and smell the starvation. Anyway, Dad got an accounting job in Manhattan when I was about two. We all moved into a little apartment, and Dad set up a desk in Mom's walk-in closet so he could write music in his spare time. Sometimes Tracy would go in there and sit and watch him. That's how he taught her to play the guitar and she taught him to play the violin."

"That's so *neat*," Sheri said, her voice dreamy, like someone she was secretly in love with gave her a present. It never seemed "so neat" before, Dad and Tracy playing guitar and violin in the closet, but listening to Sheri made it sound different.

"Yeah, I guess," I said, and looked toward the water to see if Tom was coming back. The wind shifted, and I got a whiff of his vomit. It was dark, but I could more or less smell where he'd thrown up. I started to kick sand over to cover up the spot, but Sheri thought it was better to leave it rather than risk someone stepping on it and having it squish between their toes. I nodded, even though she couldn't see, and stood there with my hands in my pockets.

"Did you ever drink enough to get sick?" Sheri asked.

I pictured the party up in Bill Moore's apartment, pictured the keg in the bathtub, pictured Allison May standing in the kitchen. "I drank enough to ask someone out." I couldn't believe I'd said it. I'd never told anyone—not even Kevin and Jimmy.

"What'd she say?"

"She threw up in my lap."

Sheri laughed. "Go away," she said, shoving me on my arm. I didn't fight it and just fell away. I'd never been shoved like that by a girl. At school I saw girls giving guys shoves all the time, but this was a first for me.

We just stood there without saying anything. Sheri was half facing me and half facing the board-walk, and I could almost see her in the light drifting down to us. She was looking at me. Or at my silhouette. We were looking at each other, my heart taking giant steps. We were sharing something. Weren't we? Wasn't this sharing some-thing? Looking at each other in the dark like this? Wasn't that sharing?

"Why don't you see if he's OK," Sheri said softly, almost in a whisper. I couldn't believe she whispered to me. Walking down to the shore, it seemed like I could've floated out over the water without realizing it. A *whisper*.

Tom was standing calf-deep in water, bending down and throwing handfuls of water up into his face. The grocery bag with the beer was tucked under his arm like a football.

"Hey!" I hollered, but he seemed deaf. Either that or I was whispering and didn't realize it. "HEY!"

Tom turned around, stumbling because he was drunk and the wet sand was holding his feet. He walked toward me. "Do you have a comb?"

"I don't *own* a comb."

"You don't? Really?" Tom sounded concerned. Apparently, he'd never noticed I used a brush—my hair wouldn't pay attention to a comb.

"Are you OK?" I asked him.

"I lost my comb." He pushed his fingers back through his hair. "Where is she? Did she leave? Oh, man, I can't believe this. I cannot believe this. She is beautiful!" Tom grabbed my arm. "Is she beautiful or what? She is beautiful."

"She's OK."

"And *nice*. She's really nice. She's so nice it's—"

"—pathetic."

"—incredible," he said, not hearing me.

"Plus her father drives an SL-nine-oh-seven," I said.

"What?"

"Nothing."

"An SL-nine-oh-*what?*"

"Forget it. I made it up. Come on."

Tom laughed and lost his balance. Then he tried to punch my arm and nearly missed.

"She's waiting. Come on," I said, turning away.

"Are you *insane?*" Tom grabbed me from the back, like he was going to tackle me. He wasn't about to throw me down to the ground, but just the way he grabbed me, I could feel how much bigger and stronger than me he was. "I can't go see her like this," he said.

"Why?"

Tom laughed again. I shrugged his arms off me and felt like swinging an elbow back at him.

"Are you insane?" he asked. "Look at me. I just threw up."

"No kidding."

"My hair's a mess. My face feels all blotchy. I look *ugly.*"

I just stared. Ugly. He was worried about ugly. I gave him a death glare, but he didn't see it because of the dark. He didn't even know I wasn't saying anything because he was too wrapped up in his hair.

"I'm walking her home," I told him, and turned around. I'd gone about four steps before Tom caught up and tapped me on the arm with the back of his hand.

"Walk between us, OK? I don't want her to get a good look."

I walked between them and had to listen to Tom apologize another fifty or sixty times. He wouldn't shut up, asking Sheri about golf, talking about football.

"Have you ever heard of Steve Largent?" he asked, looking over behind my head at Sheri. "Do you know who he is?"

"Let me guess. He plays football."

Tom bent over, laughing, and lost his balance and almost ended up landing on his head. "Steve Largent was a wide receiver," he said. "He wasn't really fast or really big or anything. But he got open. He got open and caught passes. That's what you need to do when you're a wide receiver. You don't need to be strong, you don't need to be fast, you don't need to be an incredible athlete, just as long as you can get open and catch passes."

"Sounds simple," Sheri said.

"It *is*. That's exactly right. It's very simple. Just get open——"

"——and catch passes."

"——and catch passes. That's right. If you can do those two things, who knows? That's all Steve Largent did. If you can get open and make those clutch passes when you absolutely have to. . . . Who knows? You know?"

I stared straight ahead at the boardwalk. I

couldn't believe what I was hearing—I couldn't believe Tom was talking about Steve Largent. Did Tom really think *he* was like *Steve Largent?* Did he really believe *he* was going to play professional football? And break records? I shoved my fists deep into my pockets, embarrassed. Did he realize who he sounded like? Did he? He sounded like *Dad.* Dad sounded like this. All Dad needed was two or three beers and he'd start talking about how me and Tom and Tracy could do anything. "Why *not* believe?" he asked me once, when he caught me rolling my eyes. "If there's something you want, what've you got to lose? Why *not* believe?"

Because it was crazy. No matter how drunk you were, it was crazy to think you would be the next Steve Largent. It was crazy to send your music to Bruce Springsteen. It was crazy, but that was what Dad used to do. Back when Tom and Tracy and I were little, Dad used to send out samples of his songs to Mr. Bruce Springsteen. What did he expect? Did he think Bruce Springsteen would *listen* to them? Did he think Bruce would climb into his beat-up Chevy and just pop Dad's cassette into the tape player and listen to the music as he cruised along the Jersey Turnpike? What was Dad thinking? He was a grown man.

He wasn't some fifteen-year-old kid smoking pot and playing a second-hand electric guitar. He was an *adult!* He had a job! He wore a shirt and tie to work. How did he decide to send songs to Bruce Springsteen?

My face burned just thinking about it, just thinking about Dad. No wonder he had a son who thought he was Steve Largent. What the hell. I figured if we ever got Tracy drunk enough, she'd tell us she was Madonna. And what about me? Maybe I'd think I was going to be the next Peter Jennings? Who knows what I'd think, if I got drunk enough.

By the time we reached the boardwalk, I was glad to be getting rid of Sheri so I wouldn't have to listen to any more of this Steve Largent crap. Tom didn't notice, but as soon as we got under the lights I walked around to his other side so he and Sheri could talk together.

"Boy," Tom said, smiling as he shook his head. "I can't believe you're a *Bascom* girl."

"Bottom of the barrel," Sheri said.

Tom laughed, but in a sober sort of way. We were standing outside Sheri's hotel, and he knew this was it.

"So long," Sheri said, reaching out and shaking both our hands. "Thanks for the miniature golf.

Thanks for the dollar," she said, smiling at me and then looking back at Tom. "Good luck with the team."

*Ask for her number, ask for her number, you idiot!* I kept trying to relay the message telepathically to Tom, but telepathy never works when you want it to, and suddenly she was gone.

Tom stood there. If he'd just heard I'd died in a plane crash, he would have looked happier than he did staring at that hotel entrance.

"Why didn't you ask her for her number?"

Tom looked at me like I'd reached over and nailed him on the chin.

"Now you're never going to see her again."

I could see Tom's gears turning as he thought about this.

"All you had to do was ask her."

"Shut up!" He stomped away back toward the end of the boardwalk. I went after him and eventually found him sitting at the foot of a tall sand dune, drinking another beer. I'd never seen anyone drink beer after throwing up. Was he trying to kill himself?

"She has a goofy-looking smile," I said.

"Shut up."

I didn't feel like getting sand in my pockets, so I just stood there while he drank away.

"She is really nice," Tom said.

A regular poet.

"I mean, I don't think I've ever met any-one . . ."

I looked at the lights of a ship that seemed way out there.

"I'm so *stupid!* Just—*stupid!*"

I kept looking at the ship, remembering the whisper, remembering that moment before the whisper. "Send her flowers."

"What're you talking about? I don't even know her last name."

"Tonight. Send her flowers tonight."

"How?"

"Through Phil."

"What?"

"Come on," I said, walking. "Come on. Hurry up."

Down on Main Street, next to a china-doll boutique, we found a flower shop still open. Tom was pretty stumbly and the guy could smell the beer on his breath, but he sold us two dozen daisies—my choice—and gave us a sheet of paper and a regular-sized envelope.

In the hotel lobby, Phil was still behind the desk, reading his newspaper. I swerved Tom over to the counter where there were a couple of house phones and a pen tied down with one of those ball-bearing chains, like they have at the post office.

" 'Dear Sheri,' " I said, dictating.

"Hold on." Tom's brows were knit as he concentrated on getting the letters right. He'd complained all the way back from the flower shop that he didn't know what to write, and I had said I'd tell him what to write. I glanced over at Phil, who was staring at us like he was considering calling the cops.

" 'Dear Sheri, I don't know about you, but tonight didn't work out the way I'd pictured. I had envisioned fog, candlelight, and champagne, but that's not what happened.' "

*"Envisioned?"* Tom looked up, disgusted. "I would never say *envisioned.*"

*"Imagined,* then. 'I imagined fog, candlelight, and champagne, but that's not what happened. I'm sorry. No one knows this, but I'm a closet romantic at heart.' "

"A what?" Tom pulled the pen away from the paper, like he was afraid he was going to write it down by mistake.

"Don't worry about it. Just write, OK?"

"I'm not a closet anything." He was practically screaming.

"Will you *shut up!*" I whispered, seeing Phil out of the corner of my eye walking around to the front of the desk. "All right. Just say *romantic.* 'No one knows this, but I'm a romantic at heart. All afternoon I thought about seeing your smile tonight, looking over while we played miniature golf and just seeing you smile.' "

"Slow down, slow down."

I waited for Tom to catch up. " 'To be honest, I thought it was great when you and Trish won.' "

Tom looked up at me with his mouth gawking open. "How'd you know that?"

At first, I didn't understand what he was saying. Then I remembered this was *his* letter.

"Just write, will you? 'I thought it was great when you and Trish won and you smiled, collecting your dollar from Hale.' "

"OK. Let me finish it," Tom said.

"What?"

"I want to finish the letter. I want at least *some* of it to be mine."

"Fine," I said, reaching over and grabbing the top of the page. "I'll take this."

"What're you talking about?" Tom asked,

pressing his palms down on the page so I couldn't grab it away.

"You want to write your own letter, then write your own letter."

"What's the matter with you?"

"Nothing's the matter with me. Just give me my letter."

"Hale. Come on."

"Go ahead, write your own letter. But you're not going to use this one." My hands were shaking, holding on to the page.

"OK, OK. Calm down, will you?"

I let go of the page. Tom looked at me with his mouth open, like he was wondering if maybe I should be locked up. But then he wouldn't have a letter.

"What do you want me to write?" he said finally.

"Where were we? Oh. ' . . . great when you and Trish won and you smiled, collecting your dollar from Hale. I know eyes are supposed to be what a guy notices, and your eyes are beautiful, but I don't know them, I can't read them the way I can read your smile. You have the prettiest, most suspicious lips I've ever seen.' "

Tom looked at me. *"Suspicious?"*

"You want me to spell it?"

Tom shrugged, but wrote it down.

" 'I hope you don't mind the flowers. Please don't think I'm weird. I just wanted to thank you for the great time I had tonight. The flowers are supposed to make you smile. I hope they work. Love—' " For half a second I almost blew it, but then remembered. " 'Tom.' "

# Chapter 4

*1*t worked. When we got home from our week at the beach, there was a message on the answering machine for Tom from Sheri. She wasn't sure this was the right O'Reilly residence, but she wanted to thank him for the flowers and especially the note.

Dad was at the refrigerator, putting away the ketchup and grape jelly and other stuff we'd taken to the beach, when the message from Sheri came on. He stopped and stood there with the door open, listening.

"Tom sent flowers?" he said when it was

finished. He looked at Tom. "You really sent flowers? Who *is* this girl? Are you in love?"

Matilda gave Dad a shove and told him to shush up. She'd written down the telephone number Sheri gave in the message and handed it to Tom.

"You never send *us* flowers," Dad said.

I stood at the sink, staring out the window at the weeds in Matilda's little vegetable garden. *Especially the note.* They were my three favorite words in the English language. *Thank you for the flowers and ESPECIALLY THE NOTE.*

"And I don't want *you* listening in," Dad said, poking me in the ribs like he still thought I was six.

I looked down at my ribs. "Listening to what?"

"To Tom, when he calls what's-her-name."

Dad'd caught me once listening in on the extension upstairs to Tom talking to Willy, and now I was branded. "What the——" I shook my head, getting angry in a hurry. "This is ridiculous. I didn't even do anything!"

I tried to stomp upstairs, but Dad made me come back and apologize for my attitude. He used his calm social-worker voice on me, which really bugged me because he was an accountant——he never had a social-worker voice until he learned it from Matilda.

"I'm sorry," I told him. I hated apologizing when I was in the right, but I did it just so I could get upstairs and lock myself in the bathroom. I sat on the edge of the tub and stared at the drainpipe under the sink. I should've been happy. I'd done it. *Especially the note,* she'd said. That message she left on the machine was for *me,* really. She was calling me, only she didn't know it.

That next week was the end of summer, but Sheri was still at the beach, so Tom wouldn't be able to talk to her. I couldn't stand the idea of Tom calling her up, talking to her every night, staying on the phone for hours. She was getting home Labor Day, and that Sunday night I couldn't sleep. I lay there in the dark and imagined calling her myself, disguising my voice to sound like Tom's.

"Hello, Sheri?" I tried it out, but it didn't sound like Tom, it sounded more like a jerk in a singles bar.

I didn't stick around the next day. I went on a long bike ride all the way to Marruke Park, where I could look across the Potomac and see Maryland. On my way home, I rode through Bascom.

Downtown Bascom was supposed to look like a small town, but instead of a general store and a post office there were boutiques with clothes without price tags in the windows. I stopped at The Lite Gourmet and bought a Coke and stood on the sidewalk, looking at faces of people in cars going by.

Sheri's street was on my way home, almost. I'd memorized the phone number she gave on the recording, and then checked all the Johnsons in the book and found it under Nathaniel. I didn't understand what her grandparents had been thinking, naming their son Nathaniel. On the map, it was only about a quarter of an inch over to her street, but that quarter inch turned out to be a hill that looked like a ski slope. I never walk my bike—it's kind of a point of honor—so I was out of breath and sweating like a pig when I rode by 1489.

It was a stone house set back from the road, with lots of trees and two green Volvos in the driveway. They were home. She was in there, probably, reading a book or brushing her teeth or dicing carrots. The road had leveled off, but I still couldn't catch my breath. What was she doing in there? Did she write poetry? Throw darts? Clean windows? I knew nothing about her. I had no idea what she did and what she didn't do, and before I knew it, I was past the house and coasting.

The first day of school. Tracy looked slutty at breakfast, with all that eyeliner and the short black skirt and the Ruke haircut. In Oakdale, the kids who wore black and spiked their hair or cut it crooked all hung out in Marruke Park by the river, and everybody called them Rukes. Tracy became a Ruke last year when we moved down here from New York. She was only in the eighth grade, but in the spring she started dating this tall, ugly fifteen-year-old Ruke called Mickey. Mickey and his friends were weird-looking, even for Rukes.

Tracy stared down at her bowl of cereal like she was looking for a secret code. You could tell she knew today was going to suck. It was her first day of high school, and Mickey and all her Ruke friends from middle school were going to a different high school, so Tracy was going to be on her own. I'd been through the same thing the year before when we moved down here, so I knew how much fun it was to walk around high school with no one to talk to. It was going to be even harder on Tracy, being a Ruke.

The first day of school always makes me pathetically nervous. I was OK this year until I rode my bike into the school parking lot and saw all the kids getting dropped off, parking their cars, walking in a stream of bodies toward those dark blue doors. Something inside me started jumping up and down on my stomach. I would've been all right if it wasn't for all the kids. I wished there were more short people. Or everyone had pimples. It would've been fair if *everyone* had a few pimples. Carli Anderson, Beth Morton, Tim Riddick. I always got the feeling that clear-faced people didn't think they *deserved* pimples. They washed their faces, they ate right—why would they get pimples?

Tom had given Tracy a ride to school, and I saw them in the middle of the hordes walking toward the doors. Tracy was staring straight ahead, careful not to look at anybody. I wanted to say something to her, but she'd only think I was being sarcastic.

At Oakdale you had the same homeroom all four years, so I went straight up to Mrs. Longfellow's room instead of to the quad, where everyone else would be hanging out. The room was empty—Mrs. Longfellow smoked, so she'd be downstairs in the teachers' room where smoking was still allowed. I sat in the back of the last row by the window. It was where I always sat. I hated having people behind me where they could look at my neck or my ear or the side of my face without me even knowing it.

The empty room helped me calm down. I stared out the window and thought about Kevin and Jimmy up in New York. I was thinking I actually could have enjoyed high school if I was still up there and the three of us were hanging out. We did lots of stuff together. Before Dad dragged me down to Washington, the three of us were even going to write a screenplay. Jimmy said his dad knew someone in Los Angeles we could send it to, and the three of us had joked around about flying out there and being on all the talk shows together.

"Why a duck?"

I turned and saw a girl in a black jacket with silver studs—a Ruke. She was sitting down in the seat in the other back corner. I didn't recognize her.

"Sorry?" I was always polite to strangers.

"Never mind. You wouldn't understand." She swiveled forward and folded her hands together on her desk like they'd shown us in first grade. Her hair fell across to one side and her scalp was shaved to stubble on the side facing me. *Why a duck?* Was that what she had said? I kept looking at her, wondering if I'd heard right, and she spun her head my way and stared.

"Ever try to commit suicide?"

"No." I turned and looked back out the window, ignoring her. I'd never seen her before, but I knew her type. She was one of those Rukes who tried to impress you by being outrageous. Most Rukes, like Tracy, liked to keep to themselves and pretend the rest of the world didn't exist, but a few Rukes loved to try to freak out normal people.

"You know how people who almost die think life is great?" she asked. "You know, an old man has a heart attack and afterward, if he lives, he realizes how fantastic everything is? I wonder if it works the same way with people who try to kill themselves but screw up. Do they end up thinking life is great?"

I kept looking out the window, not knowing if she was being serious or if she was about to burst out laughing. Usually when Rukes tried to be outrageous, they talked about sex or stabbing little kids or something that didn't make any sense. This made sense, at least. It made her sound like a human being.

"You new here?" I asked, facing her. She smiled. A real Ruke smile. A you're-one-of-*them* smile.

"Don't like talking about suicide?" she asked.

"Actually, I was thinking how you and my sister would get along."

"Has she committed suicide?"

I just looked at her with a blank face. "That would make her dead."

"Is she dead?"

I looked back out the window. I was right the first time; I should've just ignored her.

Other people were coming in for homeroom now and sitting down like they were exhausted. Chris Mitchell walked in carrying the same fat three-ring binder he had the year before.

"Why would I get along with your sister?"

It was the Ruke again, talking in a too-loud voice. Chris Mitchell looked over his shoulder, his eyes big, scared she wanted him to say something.

"You have the same favorite color," I said, looking out the window. I wasn't going to say anything else, but I started thinking how Tracy wasn't very good at meeting people. It took her half of last year just to meet the Rukes in middle school. Now that she looked so weird, it was going to be worse. "Her name's Tracy. She's wearing peace earrings with dangling skulls," I said, still looking out the window.

Lunch. About the middle of last year I started eating lunch with three newspaper geeks—Ronny Clark, Richie Wilson, and Sonny Prendergast. Ronny was short and looked about eight years old and never said anything. Richie always had roast beef or meat loaf sandwiches smothered in mayo, and he always ate with his mouth open. It was so disgusting they should've hired him out to fat farms. Sonny was basically OK, but he was too nice. Sometimes I wondered if he was a little stupid.

"Are you coming to the newspaper meeting this afternoon?" Sonny asked. The year before I got in trouble for missing so many meetings. Now it was kind of a joke how I figured out different ways to avoid them.

"I have a dentist appointment," I told him.

"Cindy said it's a mandatory meeting," Richie announced, his mouth full of meat loaf and mayo. Cindy White was our new editor in chief.

"Cindy's just looking for another sex toy." Her boyfriend last spring was the old editor in chief, who graduated. Supposedly they used to lock themselves in the newspaper office and push the two desks together.

Richie was still chewing his sandwich. "She's going to assign beats, she said."

A beat was what a reporter covered. I'd covered football last fall and in the spring wrote movie reviews.

"What're you saying? People are breaking down the doors to cover football? Then how'd I get to cover it last year as a freshman?"

That shut Richie up, and I tried eating the rest of my lunch without looking at him and the stuff half-chewed-up in his mouth.

Later that day Tracy walked into my geometry class. Just what I needed, my little sister in one of my classes. I knew we were both taking the same algebra last year, even though she was in middle school and I was in high school, but it never occurred to me that this year we might end up in the same class. Wasn't it illegal, having a brother and sister in the same class? Now Dad and Matilda would always know when there was math homework. And I'd never be able to blame anything on Ms. Robinson. And when Tracy went home and told Dad she got a 98 or a 99 or a 103, he'd give her a high five and turn around and ask me what I got.

"Clay says hi."

I looked at Tracy. She had her literature book out and was writing something in this organized-looking plastic folder. She was already doing her rotten English homework! That's what Tracy was like. She dressed like a Ruke and all, but she was still incredibly good at managing her time. I was doomed.

"Who says hi?"

"Clay."

"What Clay?" It really got on my nerves, watching her do her English homework.

"From homeroom," Tracy said, still writing.

I sat there for a second. "The Ruke? You're telling me her name is *Clay?*"

"It's short for Clalia."

*"Clalia?"* Where did people come up with these names? "It sounds like a disease. What's a Clalia?"

"Don't be a dork," Tracy said, looking at where she had her finger marking her place in the English textbook. I felt like telling her that true Rukes didn't *do* homework. True Rukes dropped out of high school. Then I wondered if this Clay person was a true Ruke. She was a pain in the ass; she had that Ruke attitude. I watched Tracy doing her English homework and wondered if this Clay person could end up being a bad influence on her. I kept my fingers crossed.

After school I stayed away from my locker, which was near the newspaper office, and snuck out the side emergency door that's supposed to sound an alarm but never does. I had a reputation to live up to, missing the newspaper meetings.

When Tom got home from football practice, I tried to ignore him. I knew he'd talked to Sheri sometime the day before, but I didn't really want to think about it. I hated knowing something was going on but not knowing what. Then at dinner Tom asked Matilda if he could use the phone up in her and Dad's room. It was like he was making a public announcement: *Hey, I'm calling Sheri. I'm calling Sheri, everyone!* I was about to tell him to take an ad out in the newspaper, but the phone rang.

Tom jumped, startled, and Tracy kind of flew up into the air and landed on the phone like a bomb.

"Hello?" she said, in her Mickey voice. She had a different voice for Mickey—a soft, dreamy voice, like she was about to sing him a love song. "Can I ask who's calling?"

Without even wanting to, I looked at Tom. He was watching Tracy, ready to leap out of his seat and take the phone.

"Hale," Tracy said, putting the phone down on the counter, "it's some guy named Sonny."

Sonny? Why was Sonny calling? I didn't know he even had my number. I got up and grabbed the phone. "Hello?"

"Hello, Hale? This is Sonny. I'm sorry to just call like this, but it's about Cindy."

# Chapter 5

You've got to get me a story by tomorrow morning," Sonny said. "Cindy's trying to get our first issue out Friday."

"Why?" Usually the first paper didn't come out for two or three weeks.

"She said it'll set a tone for the rest of the year."

"What does that mean?"

"I don't know. But listen, you've got to get a story in."

"Or what? I turn into a pumpkin?"

Sonny didn't say anything.

"Or what?"

"Or else she'll let Jason Albright cover football."

"Who?"

"Jason Albright. He's a new kid from California. He wants to cover the football team, and he's already given her a story for this week. It's got quotes from Coach Vincent and Brett Collard. Even Willy talked to him."

I just stood there.

"I wouldn't have even known about it except she made me the sports-and-entertainment editor. I've got to get in early before school tomorrow and do the layouts."

"And she said I needed to get a story in or forget it?"

"Sort of."

"What do you mean, sort of?"

Sonny coughed. "She said Jason was the only person on the staff who indicated an interest in covering the football team."

I stood. Stared. "I'm not on the staff?"

Dad looked up, a forkful of string beans sitting there in front of his mouth. Matilda looked over her shoulder.

"Not according to Cindy," Sonny said. "You weren't at the mandatory meeting."

I turned away from Dad and Matilda and kept

my voice low. "Did you tell her about the dentist appointment?"

"She said you are welcome to join the staff next week. We still need someone to cover the student council."

Student council? Did the paper cover the student council? I didn't even know there *was* a student council. I grabbed my forehead, pictured Cindy in a car wreck. Or a chain-saw massacre. She'd had it in for me since last spring when I walked into the newsroom and sniffed and said it smelled like sex.

"I think if you write a story by tomorrow," Sonny explained, "I'll be able to run it. Then at least you've got your foot in the door, and you can argue with her about who's covering what."

I looked up at the clock on the wall. I could write the stupid story, but what could I say. I didn't have quotes; I didn't have the roster. I hadn't even been to a practice.

"I'm really sorry," Sonny said.

"What. No problem. Thanks a lot for calling. I really appreciate it."

I hung up and stood facing the wall.

"Anything we can do?" Dad asked. At least he wasn't asking me about the dentist appointment.

"No, thanks."

Up in my room I sat on my bed. I thought about doing my laundry or cleaning my closet. I imagined folding clothes and putting them neatly away. It was a bad sign when doing laundry looked good. It reminded me of the year before, when I had to write a paper on *The Old Man and the Sea.* How much can you say about a book you haven't read?

I stood up, paced back and forth. Cindy had set me up. She knew I wouldn't go to that meeting, and she set me up. What did this Jason Albright look like, anyway? Was Cindy trying to sleep with him; was that what was going on? I looked at myself in the mirror over the dresser, turned, went back the other way. I could walk across the hall and interview Tom, but I knew what that'd be like. "I think we'll have a good season," he'd say. Or even better: "I hope we win a lot of games."

No, Tom wouldn't help. I needed something different, a new angle. I needed to interview someone famous—Gerald Ford, Paul Newman. No one famous had ever gone to Oakdale, though. I paced back and forth, back and forth. Warren Beatty had gone to Bascom. Oakdale wouldn't be playing Bascom until the end of the season, but that was still the BIG game, the game everyone'd been thinking about since they clobbered us last year. What if I could get Warren Beatty to talk about . . . I stopped. How was I going to get hold of Warren Beatty? Get his number from information out in Hollywood and hope he was home? I shook my head, pacing again. Sometimes I surprised myself, I was so stupid.

Unless . . .

I stopped again. I could call Coach Shaeffer. And Bart Bradley and Shane McDonnel. Shaeffer was the Bascom coach, and Bradley and McDonnel were their superstars. I could ask them what they thought of the Oakdale team and if they thought they'd clobber us again this year. Shaeffer probably wouldn't say much, but Bradley and McDonnel were both pretty stupid—they might say anything. And all I needed were a couple of funny lines, quotes about how Oakdale sucked and the Oakdale players spent all their time patting each other on the butt. I didn't even have to give their names; I could quote them anonymously. I could . . .

I could . . .

I sat back down, my heart beating like I was a criminal. I could quote anyone anonymously. *Anyone.* "A Bascom student," I could write. ("Name withheld to protect the not-so-innocent.

We don't want any Oakdale students getting arrested *again* for beating up on loudmouth Bascom fans.") I went over to my desk and started writing the article—I could fill the quotes in later, after the phone call. After I made *the call.*

I grabbed my notepad and tiptoed downstairs to use the phone in the kitchen.

Tom and Tracy were upstairs in their rooms. Dad and Matilda were in the den, reading. The kitchen was dark.

I left the light off and went in and tilted the phone so I could read the numbers in the light falling in from the hallway. As I dialed, I kept expecting to hear footsteps on the stairs, or Dad asking Matilda if she wanted another cup of tea. I was listening more than thinking, and suddenly the phone was ringing and someone on the other end was answering.

"Hello?"

I was expecting her dad, or her mom. I thought I'd have to explain I was Tom's little brother, but instead it was Sheri, right away, and I panicked, like I'd forgotten my lines.

"Uh . . . Hi."

"*Hale?* Is that you?" Surprised. Not thrilled, but not disgusted, either. Just very surprised.

"Yeah."

"Hi!" Enthusiastic, but with a little laugh, like this was so surprising it was funny. "How're you doing? How's school?"

"I'm—It's fine," I said, starting to answer the first question but finishing on the second. I was worried she'd think I was calling just to talk. I was embarrassed that she'd think that, even for a few seconds, and I wanted to let her know as fast as possible that this was business.

"I'm calling about a newspaper article."

"What article?"

"No article. Not yet. I mean, I've got to write an article. About the football team. And . . ." The whole idea sounded stupid now. Just incredibly dumb. I wished I'd tried it out in front of a mirror first so maybe I would've heard how stupid it sounded. Now it was too late. Sheri was laughing.

"You're calling *me* about football?"

"Yeah, I know. It was a stupid idea. I'm sorry to bother you."

"What idea?"

"No, it was stupid."

"What was stupid?"

"Don't worry about it. It wasn't anything. Listen, my dad's calling me. I've got to get going."

"Don't wimp out *now!*"

Lightning. She knew. She knew everything.

My heart was working like a fax machine, and she was reading everything on the other end.

"Tell me the idea," she said.

What idea? Oh. Yeah. The idea. My face felt feverish, but I didn't see any way out now. "It wasn't anything. I just thought I'd get anonymous quotes from Bascom fans talking about the rivalry and whatever. That's all."

Sheri didn't say anything.

"It's no big deal. I should get going."

"You're looking for incendiary stuff?"

"I don't know. Maybe. What's incendiary?"

"You want quotes that'll start a riot, right?"

"Sort of, I guess. Yeah."

"Stuff about how bad the Oakdale team is. How your quarterback throws like a girl and your offensive line has the IQ of a picket fence."

I opened my notebook and tilted it toward the light from the hallway.

"And how your receivers run like they're trying to imitate slow-motion highlights."

I was writing like crazy. "What was the one about the quarterback?"

"Wait a second. Isn't Willy your quarterback?" Sheri asked. "We should be able to come up with something good for a sleazebag like Willy."

"Why is he a sleazebag?"

"You don't think what he did to Trish was sleazebaggy?"

"Why was it sleazebaggy?"

"He has a girlfriend."

"So?"

"So did he tell Trish he had a girlfriend?"

"So did Trish *ask* if he had a girlfriend?"

"Hale!"

The kitchen light went on, and Tom stood there, looking taller than usual. "What're you doing?" he asked, walking over to the refrigerator.

My body froze, like I'd been caught, like I was guilty. I put my notepad down on the counter and kept my eyes away from Tom.

"I can't believe you said that!" Sheri hollered.

"Why'd you have the light off?" Tom asked.

"What," I said, and then realized Sheri was saying something and talked into the phone. "What was that?"

"Did he tell his girlfriend about Trish?"

"Uh . . ." I checked my notes and tried to keep track of Tom in my peripheral vision.

"Or does that not make him a sleazebag, either?"

"I don't know."

Tom poured a glass of milk and walked around

behind me. I couldn't believe I was talking to his girlfriend. I looked over my shoulder and saw him standing by the kitchen table.

"Answer the question," Sheri said. "Does cheating on your girlfriend make you a sleazebag or just a cool guy?"

"Uh . . . the first one."

Sheri didn't say anything for a second. "Is someone there?"

"Well. Yeah."

"Is it Tom?"

I felt sweat on my forehead. "Yeah," I said, looking back over my shoulder and jumping half a foot because there was this *face* right there, three inches away, reading over my shoulder. *"Get the—"* I shoved Tom with my elbow and forearm and hand—anything I could use to get him away. He was already backing up, though, and I hardly touched him.

"What's that for?" he said, pointing and laughing. "IQ of a picket fence?"

*"Da-ad! DA-AD!"* At first I was mad at Tom, but by the second *Dad* I'd remembered how Dad had warned me not to eavesdrop on *Tom's* phone call, and now Dad wasn't doing diddly about Tom reading over my shoulder. I could've had a stroke, I was so mad. I was about to start screaming my

head off about being falsely accused and what did Dad plan on doing to Tom, but then I remembered Sheri.

"Sorry," I said, glaring at the back of Tom's head as he left the kitchen. He switched off the light on the way out.

"What was that all about?"

"Nothing."

"What was he doing?"

"He tried to read my notes."

"Does he know you're talking to me?"

"Not really; no."

"Oh."

"Why?" I held my breath. "You want me to tell him?"

"What're you kidding? And ruin the fun?"

All the anger at Tom and Dad seemed to break off and drift away. I got goose bumps. She wasn't going to tell him. He wasn't going to know our secret.

"So where were we?" Sheri asked.

We talked for a long time but not long enough, and after we hung up, I stood in the dark kitchen thinking of all the things I wished we'd talked about, all the things I would've liked to have said.

Then I got a great idea.

# Chapter 6

What do you mean, I wrote her a letter?" Tom stopped combing his hair and looked at me in the mirror over his dresser. When I didn't answer fast enough, he spun around and looked straight at me. "What're you talking about?"

I knew he'd probably be all uptight about his date, but this was already worse than I'd thought it was going to be. When I was writing the letter, I'd actually believed Tom might like the idea. Maybe he'd want me to write one every week, I'd thought.

"You mailed it Tuesday," I said, not looking at him. "She probably got it Thursday."

"Are you saying . . . ?" Tom stopped himself. "What are you *talking* about?"

It wasn't until I'd tossed the letter into the mailbox outside school that I started thinking maybe Tom wouldn't be so happy about it after all. I'd decided I'd better tell him at lunch and get it over with, but when I actually saw him and Willy sitting there in the cafeteria, I thought maybe I'd wait. Tomorrow always seems soon enough when you need to tell somebody something and they're sitting there right in front of you.

That was Tuesday.

Now it was Saturday and Tom was picking Sheri up in a little over an hour and a half. If I didn't tell him now, he could end up ruining everything.

"Are you saying *you* wrote her a letter?" Tom asked.

"It was a joke," I said. Where was his sense of humor?

Tom pointed at me with his comb. "You wrote her a letter and signed my name to it?"

"What. No. I wrote it on the computer and signed it *Me. M–E.*"

"Then why's she going to think *I* wrote it?" Tom asked, raising his voice.

I shrugged. "I don't know. It sounds like you."

"You mean it sounds like *you*."

"Will you relax? I was just trying to make you look good."

"Hale—" Tom's head shook as he thought about it, and his voice got louder. "What did you say?"

"I didn't say anything."

"I want to see it."

"I don't have it," I said, and quick pulled my hands out of my pockets because Tom looked ready to do something.

"What do you mean, you don't have it? You didn't *save* it? So I could *look* at it?"

"I forgot," I said, watching his arms, his fists. Why'd he need to see it, anyway?

Tom turned and grabbed on to his dresser with both hands and took a long, deep breath. "I've got to tell her."

"Tell her *what?*"

"That I didn't write it."

I was ready for this. "What. You're going to tell her *I* wrote it?"

"So you think I care if she thinks you're a weirdo?"

72

"So you're going to tell her about the other letter?"

Tom looked at me again in the mirror and then dropped his head as he thought about it. "I don't believe this."

"It's no big deal," I told him. "Relax."

Tom didn't move. "You write her another letter, and I'll kill you."

"What time do you pick her up?" I asked. Like I didn't know.

Tom shot a look back in the mirror. "Don't—do it—again," he said in a cold, flat monotone, sounding exactly like Dad when someone was about to get grounded. Tom walked out, leaving me alone in his room for the first time in our lives. I glanced over at myself in the mirror. I knew I probably shouldn't have mailed the stupid letter, but I didn't see why it was *that* big a deal. I didn't say anything idiotic like "I love you." It was just a good letter. It was laugh-out-loud funny in parts, if you had a sense of humor. I picked up the bottle of Tom's aftershave and popped the top off and sniffed it. I thought about testing some out, but I wasn't sure I wanted to smell like Tom.

Downstairs Matilda was calling us all to dinner. Tracy's boyfriend, Mickey, was eating with us and already had his mouth full of pizza by the time I got down there. It was Matilda's idea to invite him to dinner—she thought it was good to give people a sense of belonging. I sat across from him and looked at the feather earring dangling down the side of his neck, swaying back and forth as he chewed his crust.

"Haley, could you pass the salad, please?" Matilda asked. It was only in the last week or so she'd started calling me Haley instead of Hale, and it bugged the hell out of me.

"Yes, ma'am," I said, grabbing the rim of the salad bowl with one hand and passing it toward Tom.

Across the table Mickey was bowing down toward his plate to slip more pizza into his mouth.

"How's school going?" I asked, and they all looked at me, except Mickey, who didn't realize I was talking to him until he noticed how quiet everybody was.

He shrugged a shoulder awkwardly, like he wasn't used to moving his body much. "OK, I guess."

"Good. Good," I said, nodding. Out of the corner of my eye I could see Tracy looking like she wanted to run the pizza cutter across my face a few times.

"Hale, did you say you wanted to go over to Sonny's tonight?" Dad asked, in a voice that was almost a cold, flat monotone.

I just grunted and looked down at my plate and minded my own business the rest of the way through dinner. Most of the time I didn't mind the risk of getting grounded, and I liked taking chances, seeing how far I could get. But not that night.

Riding my bike toward the mall in the dusk, everything smelled muddy like spring. It was still early September and summer hot, but the rain all day had cooled everything off and brought out the mushy smell.

I wasn't crazy. I knew it was Tom's date; I wasn't trying, in some weird, bizarre way, to make it *my* date. Sheri was Tom's girlfriend. Period. End of story. All I wanted to do was watch. I hated not knowing what was going on, and I just wanted to see where they went, what they did. Did she laugh? Did she look at him suspiciously? Did she shove him, clowning around? I didn't need to see *everything*. If they climbed into her car to make out, I wasn't about to climb into the backseat and watch. All people made out exactly the same way, as far as I could tell, and, besides, I wasn't watching them because I was some sexual deviant. I just wanted to know.

It was dark when I finally got to the mall. The parking lot was packed, and cars were cruising around, looking for parking places. I had to be careful not to get myself maimed. If I got maimed in the mall parking lot, Tom would know right away what I was doing there.

Walking into the mall, I saw Kristy Thomas and Lori Marigold coming out of some clothes store, and I quick turned and stopped in front of a window full of luggage. They were too pretty to have any clue who I was, but Kristy had been my science partner for part of last year, so she might've remembered what I looked like. Especially since she hated me because I wouldn't give her any answers. She couldn't understand it: what ugly guy wouldn't give Kristy Thomas all the answers?

A man in the luggage store came over and glared at me through the window. I probably looked like I was going to rob the place, but I stood there anyway so Kristy and Lori could clear out. I didn't want to be seen by anyone. If by some unlucky miracle anyone saw me and happened to be talking about it—say, at lunch—and

Tom was at the next table and happened to over-hear. . . . Anything was possible. I didn't consider myself psychopathically unlucky, but it was still possible. And if Tom found out I was at the mall, I might as well ride over to Marruke Park and throw myself into the Potomac, because Tom would want me to suffer before he finished me off.

I looked at my watch. Sheri wasn't supposed to get off work at Baskin-Robbins for another fifteen minutes, but I needed to find some good cover before Tom got there. Baskin-Robbins was down on the first floor, so I headed for the escalator.

After seeing her house over in Bascom, it didn't make sense to me, Sheri working in a Baskin-Robbins. I asked her about it when we were on the phone, and she said her father wouldn't give her spending money.

"Why? Is he cheap?" It's not the kind of thing you can ask when you're going out with someone, but with me it didn't matter.

Sheri laughed. "Maybe. I don't know. He says he doesn't want to see me act like a rich girl."

"Do you have to buy your own food?"

"No, food he pays for."

"What a guy."

"Yeah, he can be kind of weird sometimes. I think you'd like him."

"Yeah, right."

The whole world seemed to be watching me as I took the escalator down through the center of the mall. My eyes kept bouncing around, looking for familiar faces. It felt like an underwear dream. How do spies do it? Do they just get used to the feeling that someone's watching them?

At the bottom of the escalator, I cut over to the stores across from Baskin-Robbins and walked slowly, looking at everything in each window. Ladies' shoes, fancy coffee, jewelry, dresses, nightgowns. I kept my head down low. Out of the corner of my eye, I could see the pink sign and bright fluorescent lights of Baskin-Robbins over on the other side. All Sheri had to do was glance over; she'd recognize me right away. Good-looking people all look the same, but ugly faces are very distinctive. No one ever told me I looked like anyone. In a police line-up, I would've stuck out like a sore thumb. I should've worn a hat and sunglasses. And a mustache. I always thought I'd look better with a beard and mustache, if I could ever grow them.

King Books was right across the way from Baskin-Robbins, so I walked in fast, afraid of hearing my name. Sheri might've seen me. Even heading to the back of the store, I didn't feel safe because she might be walking behind me, ready to tap me on the shoulder when I stopped. If the store had had a back door, I would've just kept going, but instead I got to the back wall and looked at the children's books. *Snow White. Rumpelstiltskin. The Ugly Duckling.* I hated that stupid duckling story. Mom used to read it to me all the time, and I really hated it. In the second grade, I cut the pages up into snowflakes.

I took a deep breath and made my way back to the front of the store, past literature and psychology and a big self-help section. Up in front was a revolving rack of calendars that was just tall enough for me to hide behind and still get a view of Baskin-Robbins across the way. Without even looking, my eyes zeroed in on Sheri in her pink uniform, scooping a cone for a fat lady. Another girl was behind the counter, too, biting a fingernail and checking her progress after each nibble. I looked at the calendars. Women in bathing suits. Men in bathing suits. Women in negligees. I looked back across the way and saw Tom pushing his hair back off his forehead as he walked into Baskin-Robbins. I watched Sheri and thought I saw her eyes change as she looked up.

"See anything you like?"

I recognized the voice. My heart screamed. I didn't know who it was for the fraction of a second before I looked—but it didn't matter who it was because I recognized the voice so it was *someone*. Someone who knew me, someone who recognized me, someone who could tell Tom I'd been here.

# Chapter 7

**1** turned my head and went cold. Clay. The Ruke from homeroom. Tracy's new friend. Tracy who hated me. Tracy who would pay money to see me rot in hell. Tracy who would love to tell Tom anything that would ruin my life. Clay would tell her I'd been here, and Tracy would figure it all out.

"You like boobs or butts?" Clay asked.

"What?"

She was wearing the basic Ruke outfit—black everything. She pointed at a calendar of women in negligees. "A cousin told me there are boob men and butt men. Which one are you? What do you like?"

"Feet," I said, not looking at her, glancing over at the ice-cream shop, where Tom was shaking hands with the fingernail biter.

"You've never worked in a shoe store, have you?" Clay said. "That would cure you of feet. I read an article in *Newsweek* about feet. Do you know what the temperature can get up to inside a pair of tight leather boots?"

"Huh?" I was watching Baskin-Robbins, trying not to let it look obvious. Sheri had disappeared into the back.

"Five hundred twenty-three degrees centigrade. Do you know how to make the conversion to Fahrenheit?"

"Yeah. I guess," I said, peering over the top of the calendar rack.

"So were you signing autographs yesterday?" Clay asked.

"Huh?" I said, still looking. Tom was small-talking with the nail biter.

*"Huh?"* Clay said, imitating me, trying to make me sound stupid. "I'm talking about your news-paper article."

The newspaper had come out the day before, and the article I wrote quoting the stuff Sheri had said on the phone was a big hit. Everyone was reading it at lunch, and people I didn't even know were coming up and saying stuff to me.

"What newspaper article?" I asked, still watching Tom.

"Oh, get off it," Clay said. "You know what newspaper article. You're pathetic, you know that? You couldn't lie your way out of a paper bag."

"Yeah," I said, seeing Sheri come out from the back and walk around to the front of the counter. She was wearing a long, flouncy, hippie-style skirt. Now what? Think! Think! Think!

I yawned and stretched my arms out wide. "I guess I should get going home."

"You're kidding. We're not going to follow them?"

"What?" She might not have said it. I might not have heard right. She might've said something else: *We're not going to swim the Thames?* Or, *We're not growing any fall thyme?* Something else, anything else.

"Why don't we at least see where they're going?"

"What're you talking about?"

"I'm talking about your brother and his girl-friend from Baskin-Robbins. What's her name, anyway?"

I put on my confused look. "Are you making this up?"

"Look. I met your brother yesterday at school. Tracy introduced us. What's her name, anyway? The girlfriend?"

I tried to think fast but came up empty. "I don't know her name," I blurted out.

Clay smiled. "Pretty scary, isn't it? Getting caught like this."

"What. I was trying to buy a stupid calendar."

Clay just watched me a couple of seconds. "I saw you on the escalator. You kept looking over your shoulder like you were worried someone was following you. Very suspicious. It wasn't until I saw your brother that I figured it all out."

I glanced over without realizing it. Tom and Sheri were gone. I quick grabbed a calendar and looked at this woman in a see-through red negligee.

"So what's it worth to you?" Clay asked. "A shrimp dinner would go a long way toward shutting me up."

"Say whatever you want," I told her, putting the calendar back and walking by her toward the store entrance. "I don't care." I was so mad Clay had blown the whole night for me, I really felt like I didn't care what she said.

Clay caught up to me. "The real problem is, you don't know where it'll stop, do you? After the shrimp dinner, I might ask you for a leather jacket. Or tickets to Bermuda. It might *never* stop. You might be a successful banker in New York— Wouldn't you love to move back to New York? You might be making so much money you can't count it, but you won't be able to afford a new suit because I keep asking for beach houses and shiny red sports cars. All because I caught you spying on your brother."

We were walking toward the center of the mall, Clay moving sideways, facing me.

"And even if you give me everything I want, who's to say I won't decide to get mean and snitch, anyway. What would I care? So I wake up some morning and decide I don't like your face."

"Look. I don't care what you do. I really don't care." I turned the other way.

"Where's your sense of humor? I'm sorry. I went too far. So I don't know proper blackmail etiquette."

Clay wouldn't stop. She talked about how blackmail was new to her. How she'd been involved in some extortion back when she lived down in Texas, but never blackmail. Did I know she was from Texas? Tracy had told her about us coming from New York, and how I hated it down here in Virginia and wouldn't make any friends. Clay came from just outside Dallas. She started telling me about her neighborhood.

I had pretty much stopped listening when— oh, shit—I saw Tom and Sheri at eleven o'clock, walking out of a store in our direction. My stomach fell out of my insides. I couldn't breathe. I started to twist around to hide, but she saw me. First she saw me, then *he* saw me. Oh, *shit*. Sheri was smiling. Tom wasn't.

The four of us closed in on each other. I didn't know where to look. At about ten paces, Clay slipped her arm into mine. What the—? I looked at the arm, looked at Clay.

"What're *you* doing here?" Tom asked, but I was still disoriented from Clay and this arm business.

"I needed to buy a pair of rechargeable batteries," Clay said. "My dad thinks they're the greatest thing since lettuce spinners."

Sheri laughed. "I have a strange aunt who bought me a rechargeable set for Christmas," she said. "Of course, she also bought me a skin cream from Thailand that smelled like rotting broccoli."

"What," I said. "You smell a lot of rotting

broccoli lately?" I stole a look at Tom, who was watching me.

"As a matter of fact," Sheri said, "I did a science project in the sixth grade on rotting broccoli."

"Yeah, right."

Sheri looked offended, but then stuck out her hand. "Do you want to bet?" She looked from me to Clay. "He doesn't do very well when we bet."

"You two know each other?" Clay asked. I curled my toes.

"I thought you were going to Sonny's house," Tom said.

"Yeah, I was," I told him. Now what?

Clay hugged my arm. "I talked him out of it."

Tom looked at Clay and then back at me like he was trying to figure out what was what. It had to look a little strange, me with Clay and her black boots and jet black hair shaved to a crew cut on one side. I pulled my hand out of my pocket and unhooked my arm from Clay's. She and Sheri introduced themselves to each other, and Sheri talked about the beach and the bet over miniature golf. I stood there like a statue, waiting to get away. Eventually, everyone said all the nice-meeting-you crap, and Tom and Sheri were gone.

Clay stood there and brushed her palms sideways against each other like she was dusting them off. "Not bad, huh?"

"Yeah."

"Personally, I think you owe me a shrimp dinner."

"Sure," I said, walking away. Clay caught up and stared at me with her mouth open.

"You're mad at me? I saved your neck, and you're mad at me?"

"You didn't have to make it look like we were going out."

Clay just walked along beside me, staring. "You're incredible. This is incredible. This is so incredible, I don't even believe it!" she said. Then her voice got harder, almost like the girl in *The Exorcist*. "Listen, schmuckhead, it's not my fault you happen to be in love with your brother's girlfriend."

I stopped and faced her. "Look. I don't love anyone. All right? I just want to be left alone." I turned and walked.

"NO PROBLEM!" Clay called out, practically screaming, making people look. Then, even louder: "JUST STOP ASKING TO BORROW MY UNDERWEAR!"

# Chapter 8

1 should've bought her the shrimp dinner. I should've sat with her and asked her about Texas and told her about New York and how I felt like an alien when we moved down here to the suburbs of Washington. I should've gotten her an ice-cream cone and walked her home.

Morning sunlight blared through the window. I covered my eyes and rolled over the other way.

Clay was going to talk. Clay was going to get on the phone and tell Tracy everything. "Guess who was following Tom and his girlfriend last night!" I cringed. Clay would tell Tracy, and Tracy would tell Tom. And when Dad found out, he'd act like I'd stolen a car and sold drugs from the backseat.

And then Sheri would find out.

I wrapped my pillow over the top of my head, trying to keep my brains in place. "Guess who was following Tom and his girlfriend last night!" I could hear Clay saying it. Over and over, like she was sitting there in the room, trying to drive me crazy, I could hear her saying it, and I rolled from side to side holding the pillow on my head.

Then the phone rang.

I froze, listening, and heard the second ring and jumped up, kicking the sheets away and throwing the door open and hanging over the railing at the top of the stairs. I could smell pancakes.

"Hello?" Dad said, answering the phone downstairs in the kitchen. Long pause. Clay wouldn't tell Dad, would she? Would she tell Dad? I pointed my ear down the stairs and finally heard Dad, his voice sounding tired.

"I don't know what you're talking about, Meg."

*Mom!* I sighed with relief—thank you, God— and ran back into my room, threw on some clothes, ran into the bathroom. I knew Mom would call. I'd sent her a postcard about how Tracy was practically living with Mickey and Dad wasn't doing anything about it. Mom loved coming to the rescue when Dad had screwed up.

I brushed my hair, tucked my shirt in, washed the dry drool off the corner of my mouth. Mom always said I was handsome—a face only a mother could love—but even on the phone she'd nail me for walking around like a slob. Did I brush my hair? Did I wash my face? Tom was a bigger slob than I was—a lot of times he wore clothes two days in a row—but I was always the one Mom jumped on for it.

While I was giving my mouth a quick rinse with toothpaste, I went through the *what if*s. What if Mom and Dad had stayed together? What if we still lived in New York? What if me and Kevin and Jimmy still hung out in the McDonald's on Broadway?

It wasn't crazy, thinking they could've stayed together. It wasn't like something had crashed down and shattered their marriage into little shards. It wasn't one of those divorces where you *know* why it happened. There wasn't a *reason*, except maybe Dad hanging out in the closet all the time, writing music no one ever wanted. Mom didn't see the point in spending your whole life doing something you weren't successful at.

I popped out of the bathroom and ran down the stairs two at a time, wanting to hear as much as I could. Mom was in her last year of law school down in Florida, and she could talk circles around Dad with her tongue tied behind her back. Whenever they argued, all Dad could do was sit and chew toothpicks.

When I got to the kitchen, though, Dad was already off the phone, and he and Matilda were sitting at the table, whispering. Dad glanced over at me when I came in, then looked at Matilda.

Not good.

"Pancakes smell great!" I said, heading toward the pitcher of orange juice on the counter. Out of the corner of my eye, I could see Matilda watch me with her social-worker expression on her face.

"Your mother called about the postcard you sent her," Dad announced, trying to sound calm, reasonable.

I innocently sipped some OJ. "Oh, yeah?"

"She asked me to give you a message."

This was bad. Mom only gave us messages through Dad when she was really mad at us and wanted to take it out on him.

"She asked that the next time you write, you send a letter instead of a postcard."

I just stood there, facing the counter and holding my orange-juice glass.

"This way the other women she rents the house with won't be able to read about how her son thinks her ex-husband is letting her fourteen-year-old daughter dress like a prostitute."

I didn't move. Did I really write that? It sounded a lot worse out loud than it did on paper.

Dad sighed like he'd been standing up his entire life and someone had finally given him the OK to sit down.

"Don't you think it's about time you left Tom and Tracy alone and got on with your own life?"

I nodded my head. "Sure."

"Listening in on phone calls . . ."

Once! Once he caught me listening in on Tom.

"Writing to your mother about the way Tracy dresses . . ."

She dressed like a slut! It wasn't my fault.

"What's next? Are you going to have the FBI spy on them?"

My heart jumped; my eyes bounced around. I had to get out of there, had to get to a phone.

"I don't know, Hale." Dad sounded defeated. "I just don't know."

I nodded my head some more, like I could appreciate what he was going through. "Is it OK if I go for a bike ride?" I asked, turning around.

Dad was hanging his head but lifted it to look up at me, hurt. Didn't I get it? Hadn't I heard a single thing he said? Matilda reached across, gently placing a hand on his forearm, and nodded at me to go. I saw Dad look at her like she'd betrayed him, but I got out of there quick before he could say anything.

Outside, I breathed like I'd been holding my breath and ran for my bike. I had to get to a phone. I had to talk to Clay. Ask her, beg her, pay her not to say anything about last night. Dad would go through the roof if he found out I was following Tom and Sheri around the mall. And Matilda wouldn't come to the rescue, either. Matilda would talk to her social-worker friends and find out where they should ship me.

I hopped on my bike and headed for the pay phone at the Safeway shopping center. The thing was, I shouldn't have had to go racing around, groveling to Tracy's friends just so Dad wouldn't think I was nuts. I was so normal it was pathetic. Especially compared to my genius sister, who hung out with derelicts, or my paranoid brother, who ran a fever every time he took an exam. Why didn't Dad pick on them for a while?

I pedaled like a maniac up Harrison, my sleeves flapping in the wind. What if I *was* weird? I'd never really thought about it, but didn't crazy people think they were normal? How can you tell, then? If you're normal you think you're normal, but if you're weird you *still* think you're normal. I suddenly got a wave of the shivers, like when I'm alone in the dark and remember stuff that happened in some horror movie.

"Oh, give me a break," I said to myself. I knew I wasn't weird. I was normal as dirt. Period.

I got to the pay phone and called information and got into a fight with the operator. She said there were twenty-three Fiensteins, and I said there couldn't be twenty-three *new* listings for Fienstein.

"You didn't say it was a new listing, sir. I'm not a mind reader."

"Yes, ma'am," I said. I could just picture Clay calling our house while I was standing here arguing with an operator. I even expected a busy signal, but the call went through.

A man answered the phone, and I asked for Clay.

"You want who? Clay who?"

"Maybe I have the wrong number."

"You want to talk to my daughter? Is that what's going on?"

"Uh—I'm not sure."

"When do you plan on making up your mind? Ouch! Let go; I don't even know who he is yet. Yes, he. Let me ask him. My daughter wants to know who you are."

I looked over toward the Safeway, wondering if I should lie. "Hale O'Reilly."

"Hale? Who's Hale? Whoever you are, you definitely have an effect on my daughter. She looks very surprised. I can't tell if she likes you or thinks you're bull dung. My guess is it's a little of both. *Ouch!* All right, all right. Here."

I wondered if Mr. Fienstein was drunk, or if maybe he was an amateur comedian.

"What do you want?" Clay asked. "Dad. Would you mind?" Back into the phone: "What do you want?"

"I wanted to apologize." I'd figured that out on the bike ride over.

"You called me up to apologize?"

"Yeah."

"Why the rush? Why didn't you just wait until

tomorrow? You wouldn't have had to deal with my dad."

I couldn't think of an excuse. "I also wanted to ask you not to say anything."

It sounded like the line went dead.

"Hello?"

"You know, you could've said you called because you wanted to talk to me."

"That, too."

"You could really improve your lying skills, you know that?"

"I can lie OK when I have to."

"But with me, you figure you don't have to. Is that it? You think I'm easy?"

"What. I figured you'd appreciate the honesty."

The line went dead again, but this time I waited.

"What do I get for keeping my mouth shut?" Clay asked, finally.

"What do you want?"

"Tickets to Aruba."

"What's Aruba?"

"A tropical island. Why's it so important to you that I keep my mouth shut? Are you afraid Sheri will find out and never speak to you again?"

I thought of just saying yes instead of getting into the rest of it. "Actually, my dad thinks I'm crazy."

"And that's why you want me to keep my mouth shut?"

"He thinks I'm maladjusted," I told her. "If he found out about last night, he'd want to go lock me up somewhere."

"Do *you* think you're maladjusted?"

"Not that much."

"On a scale of one to ten?"

I almost said two, but I couldn't pretend to be a two. I didn't even know any twos. "Three," I said.

*"Three?"*

"Maybe a five."

"Or six."

"Maybe."

"And your parents think you're a nine?"

"Only since we moved down here."

"Oh, I get it. In New York you were normal?"

"I had a couple of friends, so I wasn't around the house as much."

"Did you have a girlfriend?"

"Yeah, right."

"You didn't have a girlfriend in New York?"

"Are you serious?"

"Was there anyone you liked?"

"There was someone I asked out once."

"Was she tall? Thin? Athletic? Beautiful complexion?"

I pictured Allison May. "Sort of."

"And what happened when you asked her out?"

"She didn't believe me. She thought I was kidding."

"And now you're in love with Sheri."

"What?"

"Who is also tall, thin, athletic, and has a beautiful complexion."

"What are you talking about?"

"I'm talking about love. You *love* her. Repeat after me. I love Sheri Johnson."

"She's all right."

"Go on, say it. I love Sheri Johnson."

"What. I like her."

"And you wish you could go out with her."

"Tom's going out with her."

"But you wish you could go out with her. Say it. I, Hale O'Reilly, wish I could go out with Sheri Johnson."

"Why?"

"Just say it! I wish I could go out with her."

"I guess maybe I wish I could go out with her; I don't know. Hello?"

Again, it sounded like the line went dead.

"Hello? Clay? Are you still there? Hello?"

# Chapter 9

1 went home and waited for Clay to call Tracy. I didn't understand why she had hung up on me, but I knew it wasn't good. I spent Sunday afternoon watching the Redskins, waiting for Dad to answer the phone and holler upstairs, "Tracy, it's for you!" I even imagined Clay had taped our phone conversation so she could play it back for Tracy over and over again, and the two of them could keep laughing until they couldn't breathe anymore.

But Clay never called. I didn't understand it. I woke up Monday morning wondering what was going on, wondering if she got into a car accident and died. It wasn't that I wanted her to die. It was just that if she was already dead, it was a good time for it to happen.

But then I thought, Did she kill herself? I remembered her talking about suicide, and I got the shivers because I could picture her actually doing it. I hoped she didn't kill herself. Thinking about the suicide even ruined the car-accident idea. The whole idea of Clay dying lost its appeal, and I was actually glad when she walked into homeroom and collapsed into her seat like it was any normal morning. I turned and looked at her. She was hanging her head forward, staring bleary-eyed at her desk, but I could tell she knew I was watching her.

"Thank you," I said.

Clay lifted her head and spoke in her extra-loud voice. "Next time you want to expose your dingdong, it's going to cost you five bucks."

Most of homeroom was there, and just about everyone looked back to see who she was talking to. I saw Kelly McNally roll her eyes at Deirdre Neeland, and Sam Milay started laughing over his shoulder.

*"Hoi-hoi-hoi-hoi,"* I imitated, making it sound even louder and more idiotic. "You sound like a pig with asthma."

Sam shut up but looked at me like he was thinking about beating the crap out of me.

I looked out the window. I should've known better than to say thank you. Saying *thank you* to a Ruke was like saying *screw you* to some guy on the football team. It was just plain stupid.

I didn't eat much at lunch. I just sat there, still thinking about how you can be weird and believe you're normal. Normal people had friends. They hung out with people they liked. I looked at Richie and Ronnie and Sonny and wondered if I could get away with honestly calling them friends. Richie was eating a salami-and-mayonnaise sandwich that half-chewed-up in his mouth looked like dried internal organs. You can't call a guy a friend when you get sick looking at him. And Ronnie never said anything, so being friends with him was like being friends with a stuffed animal.

That left Sonny. I looked across the table at him as he chewed on a carrot. He was *almost* a friend. He'd helped me out when Cindy White tried to throw me off the newspaper. Plus he was the one who talked Cindy into letting the Bascom articles become a regular thing. *And* he was the only person in the world who knew Sheri was the anonymous source. (Cindy said she had to know the name of my anonymous source before she could run the story, but since Sonny was sports editor, I got away with just telling him.)

The problem with Sonny was he was a little different. He wasn't normal. For one thing, he never seemed to look at girls. Kiki Fallows could walk by in one of her clingy, off-the-shoulder minidresses—one of those dresses that makes guys feel a little like they've been punched in the stomach—and Sonny would keep talking like nothing had happened. His eyes wouldn't even follow her butt.

He also had ex-hippie parents who named his older sister *Sunshine*. Who would do that to their kid? *Sonny* was bad enough, but *Sunshine?* I felt sorry for her when I first heard about it, but it turned out Sunshine was really pretty and smart and had a great singing voice. She was even a senior-class celebrity now because she'd gone out to California over the summer to record an album.

"How's your sister doing?" I asked him.

Sonny looked up from his carrot. "She's doing really well," Sonny said, and smiled. He'd do things like that, just start smiling all of a sudden.

After lunch I walked with him toward the science wing, worried we were going to run into Jay Dannon or somebody. Sonny had this strange way of holding his head, where it was kind of tilted to one side, and people like Jay Dannon were always making fun of him. Jay would walk right up and start a conversation with Sonny and keep nodding his head the tilted way Sonny does it, and Sonny would just talk to him like nothing was wrong. I hated watching it. I could take care of myself. Jay tried to start in on my face once, and I asked him if he had ever heard of deodorant and explained how you're supposed to use it on your underarms. It's easy to shut up a guy like Jay Dannon if you're smart, but Sonny didn't even realize when someone was messing with him.

"How do you know Sheri Johnson?" he asked me out of the blue. I looked over my shoulder, afraid someone had heard him, but who would bother listening to me and Sonny?

"I met her at the beach," I said, but then realized it sounded like I was bragging, like I was always meeting girls at the beach. "Actually, she kind of goes out with my brother."

"Tom?" Sonny asked, waking up. "She goes out with Tom?" I nodded my head, looking at Sonny. It was weird, seeing him interested in this type of gossip stuff.

"And he doesn't object to her anonymous quotes about the football team?"

"He doesn't know."

"He doesn't *know?*" Sonny asked, stopping there in the hallway and looking at me. "Then who does he think is the anonymous source?"

"This girl Trish. Look, are you going to just stand there or what?"

Sonny started walking again but was still turned in my direction. I told him about Willy and Trish at the beach and about how mad Trish got when she found out Willy had a girlfriend at Oakdale. "Tom and Willy are positive Trish is the one I'm quoting with all the nasty comments."

"When do you see Sheri? How do you meet her?"

"You think this is like spies? We're going to meet at some bathroom at the bus depot? I don't *meet* her. I talk to her on the phone."

"You talk to your brother's girlfriend on the phone, and he doesn't know about it?"

"What," I said. "You think I'm trying to steal her away?"

Sonny didn't hear the sarcasm. "No," he said, shaking his head. "It's just funny that neither of you have told him."

I shrugged. Sonny walked along, his head tilted to one side.

"Are you going to talk to her tonight?"

"I don't know. Maybe, yeah."

He kept walking, looking at the floor, and then suddenly he laughed out loud. I looked at him. Did he think *he* was normal?

After dinner I stayed up in my room, waiting to call Sheri. I pulled the screen out of my window and leaned out on my forearms, watching the sky go dark blue. The air was cooling off and I took deep breaths, picturing her answering the phone, picturing her talking, smiling, cackling. When we talked the week before, she cackled—just once, but it was enough to keep me waking up all night remembering. It sounded like her body was surprised, like it wasn't ready to laugh so loud and the cackle popped out all at once like a champagne cork.

The stars were white and clear. It seemed like I should write poetry, but I didn't feel like getting out a pencil and paper. All I felt like doing was calling Sheri and hearing her cackle. I hated waiting to call, but I kept looking out the window because waiting to call was a lot better than *after* calling. The week before, I felt so depressed after I got off the phone, I almost wished I hadn't called—which was pretty weird, when I thought about it. That was when I decided to write her a letter. It seemed even better than calling, in some ways, because I could say stuff I would never say on the phone.

This week was different. This week I wouldn't be able to get off the phone and start writing because Tom would run me over if I sent Sheri another letter. This time, once I got off the phone, that was it for the week, and I was so miserable, knowing what it was going to be like, I went down to use the phone in the kitchen and get it over with.

"Hello?" she said, taking me by surprise.

"Do you always answer the phone?"

"Hey ya, Hale!" She sounded kind of enthusiastic. "I was hoping you'd call."

My heart quit altogether. What did she mean, she was hoping I'd call? What was she talking about? Was she teasing? Was it supposed to be a joke?

"You want more quotes, I hope."

"What. You think I'm calling for my health?"

"I've got three pages of quotes here. I spent the whole week writing them down."

I looked at the kitchen doorway to make sure no one was coming. "You didn't tell Tom," I said, feeling the sweat roll down the sides of my ribs.

Ever since Sonny had talked about it, I'd been wondering.

"Didn't tell him what? That I'm your anonymous source? Why spoil the fun? I like being your anonymous source."

I swallowed. Did she do it on purpose? Did she know the way it sounded? Was she playing with my mind? Or was I just being stupid? Was that it? Was I being submoronic? She didn't mean anything; none of it meant anything. So she liked being my anonymous source. So what? So she liked being a golfer, too. She liked being tall. She liked being a girl. Big deal.

"Did Clay ever find her batteries?"

"What?" I forgot: Saturday night, at the mall. Clay holding on to my arm like we were married. It seemed like so long ago. "I don't know," I said, depressed that Sheri would think I would go out with Clay.

"What do you mean, you don't know? You were with her."

"We had a fight."

"You're kidding. What happened?"

What happened? "It's a long story."

"You don't want to tell me?"

Tell you? Didn't she get it? Didn't she

understand? Of course I wanted to tell her. I wanted to tell her everything. I wanted to pour my heart out to her in a bloody red stream. "Clay wants to date this other guy," I said.

"She told you that?"

"It's no big deal."

"She told you Saturday night?" Sheri's voice sounded like she was talking to an abandoned puppy.

"She's already been seeing him."

*"What?"*

"It's no big deal."

"Of course it's a big deal. It stinks."

"It doesn't matter." It was getting a little ridiculous, how pathetic I was sounding.

"Of course it matters. Are you OK?"

"Of course I'm OK. Why, are you sick? You have diphtheria or something?"

*"Diphtheria?"*

"It can happen, you know. Even rich people get diphtheria."

"Oh, really? And what do *you* get?"

"I don't get anything. I'm the little brother, remember. Why? What does Tom get?"

Sheri cackled. "What do you mean?"

"What do you think I mean? I mean, have you guys kissed?"

"Ha-ale!"

"That's OK. Tom already told me all about it."

"*What?* You're lying."

"He says you kiss like you're afraid of disease."

Sheri cackled again. "If he'd tried to kiss me, maybe he would've found out."

"You guys didn't kiss? I wonder why he lied about it."

"Very funny."

"What."

When we got off the phone, I went back up to my room and stood at the window. I couldn't see out because the window was closed, and the lights in the room turned it into a mirror. I looked at my reflection for a while, then didn't look at anything at all. Tom was playing music across the hall, but none of it sounded slow enough or sad enough. I walked over to my desk and sat down.

*Due to circumstances beyond my control,* I wrote out on notebook paper, *I can't send you any more letters.*

I stopped and sat and blinked for a while.

*It's weird,* I wrote, finally. *I know you're never going to read this, so I should be able to say ANYTHING, but then I think, What if I die of a brain tumor or*

*get hit by a truck, and Mom and Dad find this and
show it to you? And what if you read something in it
that makes you cringe? That's what really scares me,
picturing you cringe because of something I said, something I told you, something you found out. That's why
I can't tell you everything, even here.*

I wrote for a long time, trying to be funny
and trying to make sure there wasn't anything that
would make her cringe. And when I was done, I
folded the pages over and carefully slipped them
into the bottom of my T-shirt drawer.

It was another two weeks before Tom and Sheri
kissed, and Sheri said the only reason *that* happened was because she told herself she wouldn't
get out of the car until it did.

"So was it wonderful?"

"It was very nice."

"Nice? What do you mean, nice? Was it a real
kiss?"

"Ask your brother."

"He's not here. Was it a real kiss or what?"

"It was a kiss kiss."

"What does that mean?"

"That means ask your brother."

"So what did it feel like?"

"Ha-ale!"

"What! I'm just wondering what it felt like. I've never had a real kiss."

"You're such a liar!"

"I'm not lying. I haven't! I'm a lips virgin."

"What about Clay?"

"What about her? We never kissed."

"Right. And you're going to sell me some great swampland in Florida."

"We didn't. I'm serious. I have never kissed a girl."

Sheri didn't say anything at first. "I never know when you're telling the truth," she said. Her voice was soft, though, like she believed me, and I knew right away this was a mistake. Why did I tell her this? Why did I tell her I'd never kissed a girl? It wasn't something she'd want to hear. It wasn't something that would make her *laugh*.

"I'm saving my tongue for marriage," I said.

Sheri didn't say anything.

"Clay and I had sex a couple of times. Does that count?" I asked, and then the worst thing happened. Sheri tried to laugh. *Ha-ha-ha.* A polite laugh. A fake, tinny laugh that you use on a grandmother or a fat, pathetic guidance counselor. A sympathetic laugh. The kind of laugh you hear when some dying guy makes a speech and tries to tell a joke.

I almost hung up. I might have, except it was my own fault for wanting her to believe the truth. It was stupid, but I almost felt proud that I'd never kissed anyone. It made me different. Special. And for a few seconds there, I wanted Sheri to know that I would tell her the truth. About everything. That was stupid, though, and from then on I just asked questions about her and Tom and kept my own sex life to myself.

I actually saw her at a football game—the fourth game of the season, against Phillips. Sonny and I were by ourselves all the way up in the last row of the stands—I always stood up there and paced back and forth, watching the game—and Sheri climbed up to say hello. My hair wasn't brushed; Sonny just stood there, ogling her; and Sheri was wearing makeup—it wasn't anything like the phone calls.

"Why wouldn't you talk to me?" she asked when I called that Monday.

"What. I *talked*."

"You grunted. You didn't talk."

"I talked. Why'd you look like a slut?"

*"What?"*

"Who taught you to wear makeup like that? With the trampy lipstick."

"You're such a *jerk!*" she screamed, ready to cackle any second.

The Monday after the Martinsburg game, I noticed a difference. Sheri wasn't in a cackling kind of mood when I phoned, and when I asked her where she and Tom went Saturday night, she clammed up.

"What're you so quiet about?" I asked. "What, did you guys go to a motel or something?"

Sheri didn't say anything.

"You went to a motel?"

Sheri said softly, "No."

"Then—" But I stopped. They sure in hell went somewhere, and did something; I could hear it in her voice. I looked out the window at the dark backyard. Did they do it? Did they actually have sex? Here I was worrying about Tracy all the time. It never even occurred to me that Tom and Sheri would have sex. I couldn't imagine Tom having sex, especially with Sheri. She was a virgin. At least after the Wheaton game she was a virgin. I knew because I'd actually asked her. Had she lost her virginity since the Wheaton game? Did she and Tom actually have sex? Where? How? It didn't seem real, not with Tom and Sheri.

"It's not what you think," Sheri said at last, after I hadn't said anything for half a minute. "Not yet, anyway."

Not *yet?* Not YET? Did she realize what she was saying? Did she realize what she was doing? This wasn't funny anymore. They could get pregnant. They could have a baby.

I got off the phone pretty fast after that. It terrified me, the idea of Tom and Sheri being naked in front of each other. Having sex. I stood there rubbing my forehead. I mean, *sex!*

# Chapter 10

*W*hat's your hurry? I asked Sheri in another letter that would go straight to the bottom of my dresser drawer where she would never see it. *You know, there's no deadline for this kind of stuff.*

It didn't really bother me that Sheri wasn't going to see any of these letters, but I wanted to send her just one more that she would think was from Tom:

*Dearest Sheri,*
*No matter what I say or do, I want you to know that I care about you too much to have sex with*

*you and risk ruining your life. Even if I act like I want to, or I say I want to, please don't let us.*

*Deepest Regards,*
*Tom*

I might've sent off a letter like that if I thought I could have gotten away with it, but who would believe a guy would actually send some girl a letter like that? The problem was that Sheri was scaring me, the way she was talking. She made it sound like it was going to happen soon, maybe even that weekend. I kept trying to think of something to say to Tom to talk him out of it, but what? If the two of them were going to take off all their clothes and have sex, what could I do about it?

I closed my eyes and grabbed my forehead every time I pictured the two of them. Would they be in the dark? Or would they leave the light on and look at each other real carefully? I'd found a book of Tracy's where the girl gets up real close and practically *studies* her boyfriend's anatomy. Did girls do that? It was pretty sexy, in a way, but I prayed Sheri wouldn't want to memorize Tom's anatomy like that.

I couldn't stop thinking about it, and just to have something else to stuff into my mind, I actually started doing my math homework. It made math class a lot less painless, knowing what the hell was going on. I even answered a question once, and out of the corner of my eye, I could see Tracy looking at me.

It was kind of weird, thinking so much about sex actually happening. It wasn't that I'd never thought about sex. I *always* thought about it; it kind of lived there on a pedestal in the back of my mind. But this was different. This was the first time I thought about it really, actually *happening*. I mean, I was sort of involved in a way. Sheri never would've noticed Tom if it hadn't been for those flowers and my note. If she actually wanted to have sex with Tom—I still really couldn't picture it in my mind, but if she did, if Sheri wanted to take off her clothes in front of Tom—it was at least *partly* because of those flowers and that note. She partly wanted to have sex with me. That sounded pretty weird, and I never would've said it to anyone, or even written it in a letter that ended up in the T-shirt drawer, but it was the truth.

"Do you think about sex?"

Sonny and I were in the newspaper office. Cindy White was there, too, but you could hear the music leaking out of her Walkman, so she wasn't about to hear anything. Sonny still looked over at her, though, before he spoke.

"What about it?"

"What do you mean, What about it? Sex. The real thing. I just think it's weird, thinking so much about something you don't know anything about."

*How does it work when girls think about sex?* I had asked in another dresser-drawer letter. *Do you guys picture how individual pieces of clothing are going to be removed? Or do you just think about being with the guy in a candlelit, misty sort of way?*

"My parents think it's unfortunate kids can't learn about sex firsthand at puberty," Sonny said.

I sat there, my mouth shut. What kind of parents would say that to their teenage son? I could see what they meant, in a way, because being in the dark about it didn't seem all that healthy, but who would tell their kid that? No wonder Sonny was weird. No wonder he never looked at girls.

*If you guys ARE going to do it—if you guys feel like it's absolutely NECESSARY, I hope it's spectacular. In a book of my sister's I was reading, it was a disaster the first time around, especially for the girl. That's the way it usually happens, supposedly—sex is really rotten the first time around. But it must work great for SOME people the first time, and if you and Tom are going to do it—if you absolutely HAVE to—I hope you both get incredibly lucky.*

I stopped and bit on the end of my pen.

*But I still hope it doesn't happen.*

That next weekend, I rode my bike around all day and did math homework all night. I went to see Sonny; I did research in the library; I even went to a museum. And I prayed. God had to see sex as a sin, especially in high school, so I figured I was safe praying they wouldn't have sex. I was on the right side, at least. It wasn't like praying that Bascom's star quarterback would break his leg.

That Monday night I held my breath while dialing Sheri's number. I'd hear it in her voice, one way or the other.

"Hello?"

I wouldn't hear it in her *voice,* exactly. I couldn't tell from the *hello.* But I'd be able to tell from her mood. If she was depressed, or if she was happy in a quiet, peaceful way, they definitely did it.

"Hey."

"Haley! Hi. Listen, I'm really sorry. That's too bad about Oakdale's undefeated season."

"What do you mean?" I panicked. We'd just

won our eighth game in a row the Friday before, but had Sheri heard something? Did we have an ineligible player in the game? Did we cheat and get caught? "What're you talking about?"

"Too bad you have to play us and spoil that perfect record," she said.

I sighed in relief. I should've seen it coming. This sex thing was making me mush-minded. "Hey, I told you to stop living in a dream world," I said. "It's not healthy. You're getting things mixed up between what's real and what's fantasy."

I almost said something else to her about fantasies, but with Tom and her and this whole sex thing, it wouldn't have been funny. It didn't sound like they'd done it yet, at least. I didn't know what sex made you sound like, but whatever it was, Sheri didn't sound like it.

We discussed the article in the *Washington Post* about the game coming up on Friday. There was a paragraph in it about "an extremely popular column in the Oakdale High School paper written by Hail O'Reilly in which each week an anonymous Bascom fan insults the Oakdale team, the Oakdale cheerleaders, and the entire Oakdale student body."

Sheri tried to talk me into calling up and

complaining. "I wouldn't let them get away with misspelling *my* name."

"Yeah, right. You'd go down there and bust a few heads. You'd teach them a lesson."

Sheri cackled a little. There was a pause. "I'm going to miss these calls," she said.

I stood there on the other end of the line. It was the last Monday night of the season, the last time I had an excuse to call. I'd been so worried about this sex thing, I hadn't really thought a lot about this being the last call. Now I felt a rush of emptiness, a wave of sinking. I'd felt the same thing lots of times—watching a couple laugh with each other or climb into a car, or hearing about a whole bunch of people going to the beach together. Stuff was happening, stuff was going on out there somewhere, I could tell, and my stomach started sinking every time I thought about it. It was more than being left out. It was hearing a whole wide river of life rolling past in the dark. I could hear it, I knew it was there, but I wasn't *in* it. And it was going by. That was the worst part. It was gone. Kevin and Jimmy—they were miles downstream by now. And they'd taken the McDonald's on Broadway and the screenplay the three of us were going to write and all the laughing about anything—they'd taken it all with them. The entire city of New York was downstream. And now Sheri, who I couldn't call anymore, who would go out with Tom and then go off to college and drift farther and farther away until even if I saw her again, we'd feel like strangers.

I knew what was coming. I knew this losing-Sheri stuff would hit me again and again—when I got off the phone, when I sat down and wrote her another letter she'd never see, when I woke up in the morning, sometime next year when I heard a song they hadn't played in a while. There was nothing I could do except feel the sinking.

"I really am going to miss them," Sheri said.

"What," I said. "Of course you're going to miss them. You're going to suffer withdrawal symptoms. You're going to stare at the phone, hoping and praying it will ring. You're going to send me telegrams begging me to call."

Sheri didn't say anything for a second. "Hey," she said, finally. "Do you cover basketball?"

I swallowed. "Yeah. Sure," I said, my heart feeling like they'd slapped grease on my chest and hit me with high voltage.

# *Chapter 11*

**S**onny was late. Dad dropped me off on time, for once, but Sonny wasn't there. I squinted up at the night-gray sky, watching the fat raindrops fall into the streetlight, the wind knocking them around in different directions. I stuck my hands into my pockets, my shoulders hunched against the cold, and walked up to school to wait inside. Two men wearing police-shaped caps and shiny green raincoats stopped me at the door. They had a list of people who were allowed inside. I wasn't on it.

"I write for the newspaper," I told them. I wanted to tell them I wrote the story that Brett

Collard, cocaptain of the football team, had held up in the air at the pep rally, the story that got everyone screaming and cheering and chanting, "OAK-DALE, OAK-DALE, OAK-DALE." I wanted to tell them I was practically famous now, but I knew it wouldn't matter to them without my name on the list.

"Clear the way," the tall one said, brushing me aside with his arm as the one with the mustache opened the door for a stream of cheerleaders in their bouncy white skirts. Some of the cheerleaders had umbrellas, but most of them had taken off their jackets and held them over their heads, as if freezing to death was OK as long as their hair looked right.

"I didn't see you checking *their* names off the list," I said.

"What're you, a lawyer?" the tall one asked.

"Come back in a cheerleader uniform and maybe we'll reconsider."

They both laughed, tapping each other on the arm with the back of a hand.

"You guys should be on Letterman," I said, and walked away before they decided to arrest me. Mr. Pollinger, our principal, had gotten on the PA that morning to talk about all the police there'd be at "the big game tonight." He warned us that no disorderly behavior would be tolerated and that the police were instructed to make arrests at the slightest provocation. Walking away, I kept expecting these two cops to grab me from behind and start reading me my Miranda rights.

I stood under a streetlight at the edge of the parking lot, the rain soaking through my hair like I was taking a cold shower. Dad had told me to take an umbrella, but Sonny always carried around a green golf umbrella, so I'd figured I'd be OK. Where was he, anyway? He has one of those watches that keeps track of the hundredths of seconds. He was never late. Did he try driving himself? We both had our permits, but it'd be another miserable year until we actually got our licenses. Did Sonny try driving, anyway, and get into a car accident or something?

The parking lot was already filling up, which gave me butterflies about the game. It was good Sonny was late, in a way, because at least being mad at him was distracting. After a while, though, I started to worry. Lots of ugly-looking things could happen in a car accident: cracked heads leaking blood or bones sticking through blue jeans. I was good at picturing incredibly awful stuff. Eventually, though, Sonny's sister showed up in her old VW Bug and splashed to a stop. The windshield wipers kept going as Sonny climbed out, and I looked at Sunshine sitting there in the driver's seat. She really was beautiful, which was lucky because an ugly Sunshine would have been in real trouble.

"What's that smell?" I asked, after Sonny and I had ducked under his umbrella.

"What smell?" Sonny was combing his hair. He looked like a little kid, the way he held the comb in the middle with the palm of his hand and pulled it across the top of his head. I leaned toward him and took a sniff.

"Is that cologne?"

Sonny laughed. "Is it bad?"

"What. It's fine. I don't care," I said, shrugging, looking at him and trying to remember if I'd ever seen him with a comb before.

Inside the stadium, the bleachers on the Bascom side were already packed. All the people over there wore red and white and clapped and jumped up and down like they'd been locked up for three days. The stands on our side were four times taller, but they were getting full, too. Sonny and I climbed up to our normal spot—last row, fifty-yard line. From the railing at the top, I could look out over the parking lot behind the stadium. It was full, and hundreds of people who must've parked somewhere else were walking across it, sliding between parked cars, adding to the crowd bottlenecked at the stadium entrance. I felt the butterflies again and started pacing back and forth. I never enjoyed watching a game Tom was playing in unless we were up by three touchdowns, and we'd never be up by three touchdowns against Bascom. I took a deep breath, still pacing.

"Something bad's going to happen," I said.

Sonny lifted his umbrella to look out at me. "Like what?"

"Like if I knew, I'd tell you."

People kept pouring across the parking lot, and eventually our row filled up, so there wasn't any room to pace. I got back under the umbrella, feeling claustrophobic. I resented all these people being here. Where were they for the other games? Why let them in now if they hadn't bothered with the other games?

We kicked off. Bascom returned it to the twenty-seven.

"We're going to lose," I said. "I really have this feeling we're going to lose."

"You always have a feeling we're going to lose."

We stood there and watched. Two-yard gain. Four-yard gain.

"We've got to stop them here," I said, but Sonny didn't say anything. He knew enough to keep his mouth shut, to leave me alone. Bascom tried to run it into the middle, but we pushed the whole line back. So they ran it around the end, instead, for sixty-five yards and a touchdown. I looked at Sonny, mad at him for that crack about me always thinking we're going to lose, but then the man to my left started clapping and stuffing his fingers into his mouth to whistle.

"Way to go, Shane! Way to go!"

I stared at him. I knew he could tell I was staring at him because he wouldn't look at me.

Bascom scored another touchdown at the end of the first quarter, and Mr. Jerk-to-my-left started jumping up and down like some idiot who had won the lottery. I wanted to hang him by his feet over the railing. *Jump up and down now, sucker. Go ahead.*

They added a field goal with three seconds left in the half. I couldn't take it anymore. "I'm going home," I said.

"What for?" Sonny asked.

I looked at him. "I forgot my sunglasses. What do you think, what for? I don't feel like watching us get our butts kicked."

"What if we win?"

"Not to worry," I said, and fought my way down through the crowd, imagining everyone was a Bascom fan and pushing them out of the way. At the bottom of the stands no one could even move. It felt like being on the subway at rush hour, and I kept expecting some woman to turn around on some guy and call him a pervert. The police stood in rows, not even trying to direct traffic. I could smell wet wool and mud, and I just inched my way along with everyone else, minding my own business.

"Hey, loverboy!" It was Clay, appearing from nowhere and punching me on the arm with the edge of her knuckles.

"Hi," I said, rubbing my arm. Clay must've caught me right between the muscles because it really hurt. Her hair was wet and straggly and pretty normal-looking. It'd be hard to tell she was a Ruke just by looking at her.

"How's that broken heart doing?" she asked.

"What? Great." I didn't know what she was talking about, but something was going on; I could hear it in her voice.

"Takes a licking but keeps on ticking, huh? Do you remember that commercial? I used to love commercials that rhymed. I thought they were poetic."

Clay sounded like a prosecuting attorney who just found that last piece of evidence that was going to put me away for life. Now she was going to have some fun; she was going to play with me for a while.

"So tell me about this guy," she said.

I kept looking at the back of the head of the lady in front of me, acting like I didn't realize Clay was talking to me. Guy? What guy? I had no idea what she was talking about. Or why she sounded so happy.

"He sounds like quite a dish," she said. "A guy can be a dish, can't he?"

"Sure," I said, not looking at her. She sounded so cheerful, it was scary. Did Tracy tell her something incredibly embarrassing? Something I did when I was little? The time I took off my pants in Macy's?

"Say! He's not on the football team, is he?" Clay asked. "Is he on the football team?"

"Who?" I asked.

"Who do you *think*? Him!"

Maybe she was making the whole thing up. "What's his name?" I asked her.

"That's what I was going to ask *you!*" she said, and punched me on the arm again in the exact same spot. My hand went tingly, like it was paralyzed. "I was sure you knew his name. Or didn't you plan that far ahead?"

What was she talking about? I tried to think. This was like one of those algebra word problems—I just needed time to think. I was great at word problems if I had time to think.

"I'm disappointed in you," Clay said, over-doing it on the fake sincerity. "I would've thought you'd have had it all planned out. Who he was. What he looked like. How many chin-ups he could do in gym class."

If she would've just shut up for fifteen seconds, I could've figured out what she was talking about.

"What if she'd asked you his name? Or what year he was in? What would you have said?"

*Blam,* it hit me. Oh, shit. She'd seen Sheri. Sheri had said something to Clay about breaking up with me for that other guy. Now Sheri knew I'd lied to her.

"Hey, am I still a virgin?" Clay asked. "I've got to know. Has he devirginized me?"

We were still locked in the crowd, and Clay was practically screaming. The lady in front of me looked back when she heard about virginity. First she looked at Clay, then at me. That really got Clay going.

"My dad's going to be very upset if I've been

devirginized. You should never be devirginized by a boy when you don't even know his name."

"Woodrow Wilson," I said, looking down at my sneakers. "He's a freshman. And a homosexual. But you love him anyway."

Clay didn't say anything for a while. I thought I could see her out of the corner of my eye, looking at me. Then she started poking my arm with her finger. "Sheri—doesn't—think—you're—very—funny."

*"Will you knock it off? That hurts!"* I held the palm of my hand over my upper arm like a bandage.

"She thinks it sucks you lied about me. I think it sucks, too. We both think it sucks. We had a nice long conversation about you. I told her the real problem is you didn't want her thinking you were going out with *me* because you were in love with *her*."

The lady glanced back over her shoulder. Now she was smiling. It was funny. A joke.

I looked at Clay. "Give me a break, will you? I'm not in love with her."

*"She* thinks you are."

"Who?"

"Who do think?"

"Sheri said she thinks I'm in love with her?"

"So is Woodrow coming with me and Tracy on the art trip next weekend? If he's gay, he must love art."

Some art teacher had hired a bus to take kids up to New York for the day. Tracy and Clay had already signed up.

I couldn't have cared less. "Did Sheri say she thought I was in love with her?" I was getting mad at Sheri, just thinking about it.

"Hey, maybe you should come, too. You could show Woodrow around New York. He might like that."

"Did she really say I loved her?" It seemed weird, saying the word. I felt like I was admitting something.

"Unless you're worried about what Woodrow would do to you."

*"Did she say I loved her?"*

"Do you?"

We'd gotten to the stadium entrance. The crowd was breaking open, but I didn't move. "Look, could you just stop being so *cute* and tell me?"

Clay's face changed, like I'd shot her. Like I'd stuck a gun in her ribs and fired away and any second now blood was about to spill out of the corner of her mouth. I almost actually reached out to hold her up. She looked different, like a different person. A normal person, with human emotions.

"Clay, I didn't mean——"

It didn't matter. It didn't matter what I meant; Clay had turned, pushed through the crowd, and was gone.

"I'm sorry!" I said, and then screamed to make sure she heard. *"I'm sorry!"* People stared, but I just gave them a screw-you look and stood there with waves of bodies streaming past. Was Clay really that upset? She had looked like she might cry. Was she really going to cry?

I stood there. I didn't feel like going home now and thinking about Clay all night, so I turned back toward the stands. All I'd said to her was "stop being cute." What was so bad about that? I said meaner stuff to her in homeroom all the time. Why did her face, all of a sudden, have to go normal on me *now*? Was she having her period? It wasn't that mean, what I said. I'd never seen a face change like that. It was like suddenly she was a human being, a girl.

It felt strange to think of Clay as a girl. Was she really a virgin? All that devirginize crap, was she just making it up? I'd never thought about Clay being a virgin or not being a virgin because

I'd never really thought of her as being a particular sex before. Did she have a boyfriend? It was hard to tell with Rukes because they all hung out together, like a pack of dogs.

I spotted Sonny's green umbrella still there in the last row and started climbing back up into the stands. I couldn't imagine Clay crying. It'd be like seeing Arnold Schwarzenegger crying. Could *his* face change like that? All because someone asked him to stop being cute? Wasn't it a little crazy, in a way? Getting so bent out of shape? It didn't make sense, having convulsions like that because someone said to stop being cute.

I got to the top of the stands, but it was the wrong umbrella. It was big and green, but there was a girl underneath it, all by herself. I looked for another umbrella.

"Are you Hale?"

"What?"

It was the umbrella girl. She smiled at me with her head bent sideways, like she was trying to read something upside down.

"Sonny should be right back," she said.

I looked at her. My stomach fell over the railing.

# *Chapter 12*

1'm Laura Nickels," she said. "Sonny went to get us hot chocolate, but the line looked about three miles long."

"Oh."

"Do you want to share the umbrella?"

"No, no. That's—No, thanks." I just wanted to get away. Anywhere. As fast as possible. I felt pathetic standing there with Sonny's date. This was his date, right? He didn't have another sister, did he? A cousin? I almost asked, but then I remembered the cologne. And the comb. Holy shit. Sonny had a date.

Laura pointed at me. "We had history together last year, but you probably don't remember. You sat in the back by the window, and I sat in the front by the window. I never said a word, so you probably didn't even know I was there."

"What. No, I remember." Her face looked a little familiar, like I'd seen her in a commercial a long time ago.

Laura said she and Sonny had been planning on meeting after the game, but when I left, Sonny went and found her with her friends.

"Are you going to the dance?" she asked, all bright and upbeat.

"I don't know," I said. I hadn't known there *was* a dance. Was it here at school? Tonight? How did they advertise that stuff?

I stared out at the field, like the most important thing in the world to me was watching the Bascom team run over to their sidelines for the second half. Sonny had a date. He was taking this Laura to the dance. The dance he never even *mentioned* to me. I couldn't get over it that Sonny had a date. I felt dazed, like when I was a little kid at the ocean and I'd get lost in a wave and then suddenly be slammed down on the beach with the slushy, sandy water rushing back out to sea. Sonny had a date. It was like a priest having a date. It'd never even occurred to me he'd *want* a date. Was he going to kiss her? Was Sonny actually going to kiss a girl? I couldn't picture it—I couldn't picture Sonny tongue-kissing some girl. He'd just never do it. He'd just stand there, too embarrassed to do anything, until someone wheeled both of them away to the nursing home. A girl would have to beg him to kiss her. Was Laura the type? Would Laura beg Sonny to kiss her? She looked shy, but who could tell? She might beg.

"There he is!" she said, pointing. She sounded so excited, I wanted to throw up. I looked down and saw Sonny, a jumbo Styrofoam cup in each hand. It looked like his lips were moving, and for a second I thought he was singing or talking to himself, but then I saw the eyes behind him, staring up at me.

"Shit."

"What's wrong?" Laura asked.

"What. No, I was just . . ." I didn't know; I couldn't think. I looked left and right, but there was nowhere to go. My heart was beating too fast, and I quick—without realizing it—ran my fingers back through my soaking-wet hair, probably making it look even funnier. It was Sheri walking up the stairs behind Sonny, staring up at me. I couldn't believe this. I couldn't believe how un-lucky this was. First she runs into Clay, and now this.

Sheri's lips moved, and Sonny looked up and smiled. I should've gone home. Why didn't I go home? Sonny tried to wave with his right hand, but the Styrofoam cup made it look like he was making a toast.

What was Sheri doing here, anyway? Why wasn't she watching the game from over on the Bascom side where she belonged? She was wear-ing a light blue raincoat with a loose hood. Her skin looked really clean, like she was doing a soap commercial.

When they reached us, Sonny introduced Laura and Sheri to each other, and they both acted like they were really happy they had the oppor-tunity to meet. Then Laura offered Sheri her big Styrofoam cup of hot chocolate.

"This is plenty for us," she said, pointing to Sonny's cup. "You two have that one."

You *two*? Did she say "you *two*"? Did she think Sheri and I——? That we went around, sharing hot chocolate? Was she blind? Did she think Sheri was blind?

Sheri turned my way, holding the cup at a

threatening angle, ready to dump it all over me. "Want some hot chocolate?" she asked, her eyes open wide in a crazy-person glare.

"No, thanks," I said, my hands up.

"You sure?" she asked, moving the cup toward me like it was a knife.

"Positive."

She sipped from the cup, still watching me. "I guess I don't have to tell you who I met down in the girls' room."

I pointed at the field. "Good game, huh? You guys are really kicking our butts. That last touchdown drive was incredible."

"I was rude to her. Clay didn't understand. I wouldn't even talk to her because I thought she'd been a jerk to a good friend of mine."

"What, you mean breaking up with me? Did you think I was *serious?*"

"Don't—even—try it."

"What," I said, but then cracked up because Sheri just kept scowling. "I like that hood, by the way. It's very—It's big, you know? Kind of makes you look like a rabbit."

Sheri stared. "Don't."

"What's the big deal? I'm serious. What's the big deal? So I'm a jerk."

"You are."

"I know. But look, at least Tom's not a jerk, right? That's what's important. You're not going *out* with a jerk. You just know one. So big deal; everyone knows jerks. They're all over the place. Life's lousy with jerks." I reached over and pulled her hood down.

Sheri looked at me and pulled the hood back up on her head. "Clay has some really bizarre ideas about you, you know that?"

"Clay belongs in a loony bin," I said, looking down at the field, afraid to look back at Sheri.

"Do you know what she thinks?" Sheri asked.

"She's a nut," I said, still watching the field, not moving my eyes, feeling my heart going like mad. "I'm serious. She's like totally deranged." I didn't know what I was saying, but I wasn't going to stop. "Her brain cells must have a missing chromosome or something. A deformed synapse. I read an article about that stuff. It's weird. It's really—You should read about it sometime."

Sheri didn't say anything. I didn't look at her, even out of the corner of my eye, afraid she was going to ask, afraid it was going to show. I was pretty sure Clay's bizarre idea was that I was madly in love with Sheri. It was awful, that Sheri might've heard Clay say that, but my heart kept beating like it was exciting, too.

In the third quarter, when Bascom kept getting first downs, it didn't bother me. We were already losing 17–0 and didn't stand a chance, anyway. Losing this way was easy, relaxing. Even when we intercepted for a touchdown, I still felt relaxed.

"We're still going to lose," I told Sheri, and pulled her hood back again.

Midway through the fourth quarter, we drove the ball down to the six-yard line, and Willy hit Tom in the back corner of the end zone. I didn't feel relaxed anymore. It made me mad, in a way, because they were just getting my hopes up. I still knew we weren't going to win. There was no way we'd win, I knew it, and then we missed the extra point. *See,* I almost said. *What'd I tell you?* I looked at the scoreboard, at the 17–13.

"We're still going to lose."

"It's nice, the confidence you have in your team," Sheri said. I pulled her hood down again. This time she just left it.

Nothing happened for eight minutes. Bascom punted with 1:37 left, and we got the ball on our own thirty-five. People were screaming and stomping their feet, and the stands felt like they were going through an earthquake. We ran the ball for sixteen yards, then threw for twenty-two, and ran for another fourteen.

Time out. Eleven seconds, ball on the thirteen. Willy walked over to the sideline like he was strutting down the boardwalk on a Saturday night. He loved this kind of thing. Willy was the type who'd like to spend his vacation with eleven seconds left and the ball on the thirteen. I looked out at the huddle, where Tom must've been ready to throw up. He hated pressure, hated not having enough time, hated exams even when he'd studied and knew all the answers.

"How many time-outs do you have?" Sheri asked, looking at the scoreboard.

"None."

"*None?* Are you sure?" She sounded panic-stricken. I stared at her, suddenly realizing: she was rooting for us. She glanced my way and then turned and held a hand in front of my face. "Don't look at me like that. I can root for whoever I want."

I just kept looking at her.

"Stop it!"

"Sheri. I think it's nice, OK?" I didn't know what to do. "Here. Put your hood up." I pushed the hood back up on her head. Sheri turned and looked at me. I could just see part of her face past the side of the hood. She looked ready to say something serious, which made my heart feel like it was falling down a flight of stairs.

"What," I said, pointing to the field. "Now you're not going to watch?"

Oakdale broke their huddle, and the stands cheered like we'd already scored. I watched us run up to the line of scrimmage, picturing Sheri's face just past the edge of her hood, the serious expression in her eyes. I loved making her laugh, loved making her cackle, but it was nothing compared to that look.

Willy walked up and bent down behind the center, who hiked the ball almost right away. It all looked slow-motion in the rain. Willy began to drop back to pass, but two Bascom players ran through the line, unblocked, and one of them jumped and grabbed Willy's jersey. If Willy had gone down, time would've run out and the game would've been over, but he shook the guy off and went running for the sideline with three guys chasing after him. Sheri grabbed my arm and squeezed tight. Willy went out of bounds at the eleven to stop the clock with two seconds left.

Sheri and I looked at each other but didn't say anything.

Laura kept cheering. "You can do it, Oakdale! You can do it!"

I knew she was wrong. I knew we wouldn't do it, but I kept my mouth shut and clapped and stomped my feet along with everyone else. Sheri grabbed my arm—the same arm Clay kept punching—as soon as we broke the huddle.

Willy hiked the ball and rolled left to avoid a lineman charging at him. Two more Bascom players streamed through, and all Willy could do was heave the ball toward the end zone. Toward Tom. I could see his number on the back of his jersey. Turn around. Turn around! Sheri squeezed my arm like she was trying to break it. The ball was in the air, it was coming down, coming down, but Tom wasn't looking, wasn't looking, but then he turned back. He turned back and—incredibly, instinctively—threw his hands out for the ball. Threw his hands out for the ball and—unbelievable miracle—got his hands underneath the ball, the ball—INCREDIBLE!—falling in his hands, falling right into his hands, and falling right through his hands and still falling, falling into the mud.

# Chapter 13

H ere," Sheri said, handing me her car keys. "Don't give them back to me. Even if I threaten you with a golf club."

The bathroom door opened, and Karen Simpson tiptoed out, looking like she was trying to keep her head from falling off. Sheri slipped in, waving to me as she closed the door. Was I getting her drunk? Was I *trying* to get her drunk? Was I trying to get *me* drunk? I drank some beer and looked at the car keys in my hand and shoved them into my pocket. We weren't completely drunk. We weren't stumbling around; we weren't throwing up. But we were definitely drunk.

"Damn drunk," I said, and laughed because it was funny.

I looked at my watch, then over toward the door. Still no Tom. He'd given Sheri directions and said he'd meet her here, but it was before the game when he said that. Before he dropped the ball. Before he ruined the season. Driving over here, I told Sheri that he wouldn't show.

"He's not going to want to see anyone. Especially you."

"Thanks a lot."

"What. He thinks he lost the game."

"How? He didn't even see the ball coming."

"He's going to think Steve Largent would've caught it."

"Who?"

"He's not going to want to see you," I told her. "He's not going to want to go around laughing and dancing and kissing."

Standing outside the bathroom, I wondered how much they kissed when they were together. Did Sheri like the way Tom kissed? Was it something she looked forward to?

I looked back over my shoulder, toward the door. Tom wouldn't want to have fun because then he might forget, and he'd think it was wrong to forget. He'd think that since he dropped the ball, since he lost the game, the least he could do was remember. He wouldn't be able to think about anything else because he wouldn't *want* to think about anything else.

"He's crazy," Willy had said when he showed up at the party with a bunch of guys from the football team. "There's no way he should've caught that. It was a miracle he even got his hands on it. I just wish he'd never turned around in the first place, so he couldn't blame himself."

Now Tom was off somewhere, still turning around, still throwing out his hands, still seeing the ball roll off his fingers. Over and over and over again.

Light spilled out as the bathroom door opened.

"Let's dance," Sheri said, her mouth almost in my ear. It was the only way you could hear over the music. I shook my head.

"I don't dance," I said, but Sheri grabbed me by the wrist and pulled me toward where people were dancing. Her palm was warm, but her fingers were cold. I looked to see if anybody was watching, because the way Sheri had my wrist, it almost looked like we were holding hands. It was tough to see anything, though, in the crowded dark—the party was packed into Bill Lockett's basement, and Bill'd gone around licking his fingers and unscrewing lightbulbs. Probably no one could see Sheri had ahold of my wrist, even if they were looking.

"Sheri. *Sheri*." I was hollering, but she kept pulling me through the crowd like a tugboat. I stopped before we made it to the people dancing, and finally she looked back.

"What's the matter?"

"I don't dance."

Sheri leaned over. The music was even louder here. "What?"

I hollered again. "Tom's going to be here soon!"

Sheri hollered back. "I thought you said he wasn't coming!"

"He might!"

"So?"

"So dance with him!"

"So when he gets here, I will!" she said, and then just looked at me. She looked at me seriously, like I was a human being, like I deserved being taken seriously. I couldn't swallow.

"I'm going to get a beer," I said.

Sheri looked at her cup and nodded. We headed for the keg on the other side of the basement, where it was a little quieter.

"Why don't you dance?" Sheri asked, once we got on line.

"It's just easier," I said over my shoulder. Sheri walked around and got in front of me on line and turned around to face me.

"Easier than what?"

"Easier than having these girls hanging all over me, begging me to dance."

Sheri just looked at me straight on, her face about eight inches away. I'd never seen her skin so close.

"How many beers have you had?" I asked, backing away.

Sheri laughed. "Why? Do I seem drunk?"

"I don't know. You're drinking like a fish, though."

"What're you talking about?" Sheri looked at me with wide-open bug eyes. "What about you? Why are *you* drinking like a fish? You don't even drink. That's what you told me at the beach. You said you promised yourself you'd never drink again."

I looked at her, surprised, happy she remembered.

"What made you start drinking tonight?"

"I asked you first," I said, and Sheri looked

at me. She stared the way drunks in the street stare when they don't know what to do.

"I think I wanted to know the truth about something," she said, finally.

I could barely breathe. "About what?"

"Get out of here! What do you think, I'm stupid? First you've got to tell me why *you're* drinking so much."

"What. I'm thirsty."

Sheri shook her head.

"What."

"Hale. If you want me to be honest, you have to be honest."

"I don't care if you're honest. If you want to lie, that's fine with me."

"What made you start drinking tonight?" she asked again.

It was really hot in there, and I wiped some sweat off my forehead. "I don't know. Maybe I wanted to think anything was possible."

"Like what?"

"Like anything. I don't know."

Sheri just kept watching me. We got to the front of the line and poured our foamy beers and walked over to a wall with a big diamond-shaped orange road sign saying Construction Ahead. Bill

Lockett was the kind of guy who ripped off road signs. He could probably supply a small town with a complete set. I was embarrassed now and couldn't look at Sheri, so I kept rereading Construction Ahead a couple of hundred times. Out of the corner of my eye, I could see Sheri sipping her beer, looking at me.

"Did your brother ever tell you about the letters he wrote me?"

My heart didn't know which way to turn. "About the what?"

"He wrote me a letter the night at the beach and another one the first week of school. Did he ever tell you about them?"

"He's going to tell his little brother?"

"He might."

"Yeah, right. And he also told me about the first time the two of you had sex."

Sheri's mouth dropped open—or started to drop open. She recovered in a hurry, sort of hiding a smile, and I couldn't tell if the original shock was because Tom had told me they'd done it, or because she couldn't believe Tom had *claimed* they'd done it.

"He said it was great," I told her, "but you seemed a little disappointed."

"You're a strange character, you know that?"

"He said he'll make up for it next time."

Sheri looked at me sideways, her mouth ready to smile but not quite doing it. "Tell me about the letters."

"What letters?" I asked. I couldn't remember how much she'd told me, and I knew from TV that that was the way people got caught—they said things they weren't supposed to know. "Tom gave you letters?"

"He dropped the first one off," Sheri said, watching me, "and mailed the other one."

"Mailed it where?"

"You're really a bad liar, you know that?"

"What."

"You're not bad when people aren't expecting it, like the junk you told me about Clay dumping you, but the smoke screen you're trying now is ridiculous. It's not working at all."

"Smoke screen about what?"

"You're so transparent," Sheri said. "I can see right through you."

"Good. Great. Wonderful. I don't need to talk then, right? I'll just stand here, and you can tell me what I'm thinking."

Sheri kept smiling a drunk smile. "Those letters changed the way I thought about Tom."

"So why're you telling *me*?"

"They made him seem different from anyone I'd ever known."

I nodded but looked away, like I was getting bored. I couldn't see anything, though, because I was concentrating too hard on trying to listen.

"When I left you guys on the boardwalk, I didn't even give him a second thought. But then I got that first letter and I told myself, OK, the guy deserves a chance. So I called and we talked and it was nice. Then when I got the second letter . . . I couldn't get over that second letter."

I kept my head turned away, my eyes not focusing on anything. Why was she saying this? Was she doing it on purpose? Did she want me to tell her? Was she trying to find out?

"Hale?"

I pretended not to hear.

*"Hale?"*

I kept my head turned away but looked at her with my eyes.

"Did you?"

"What."

"They sounded like you."

"Grab this for a second, would you?" I asked, holding out my beer cup.

"Not until you tell me."

Leaning down to put my beer on the floor, I

lost my balance and bumped my head against the wall. I wondered if maybe I was a little drunker than I thought.

"Why won't you tell me?"

I stood back up and felt my whole head tingle. I had to just stand there until the tingle drained out.

"Hale. Why won't you tell me?"

" 'Cause I think I'm going to throw up."

"Don't give me that."

"No, I'm serious," I said, reaching out to hold on to the wall.

"You're not going to throw up and you know it."

"I'll be right back."

"Let me give you some advice. Don't ever try to be an actor. Hale. Hale, wait!"

I stumbled away toward the door to the side yard. I thought I was doing a pretty good job, no matter what she said. How'd she know I was pretending, anyway? I was pretty drunk. I was *close* to throwing up. What tipped her off? And why was Sheri doing this? Why was she trying to find out about the letters all of a sudden? Was it true, that crap about the letters making Tom seem different from anyone she'd known? I didn't believe it. What'd I say in the stupid things? I couldn't remember exactly, but I didn't think there was anything *that* tremendous. I half wanted to go back and ask her what exactly about the letters was so tremendous, but by then I'd made it to the door and yanked it open.

Outside, Don Stewart and Kiel Galworthy were leaning against the house, making out. They were really into it and looked about ready to tear their clothes off. The air was cold and a gust held my breath like I'd jumped into ice water. I went over to use some dark bushes that guys had been using all night for a bathroom. The sky had cleared after the rain, and I looked up at the stars. *Different from anyone I'd ever known.* It sounded like a famous line in a movie, and I wished I had a notebook so I could write it down. *Different from anyone I'd ever known.*

"That's me," I said, and laughed for no reason. Why'd she want to know who wrote the stupid letters, anyway? What was the point? Even if I'd told her that I *did* write the letters, then what would've happened? Would she have leaned over and kissed me? On the lips? Would she have put her arms around me? And held me close? I looked over my shoulder at Don and Kiel, still going at it. Would she have done that? With me?

For half a second I thought—maybe. Who

knows? Maybe. Maybe if I told her about all the other letters. Maybe if I took her up to my room and showed them to her. Maybe . . . My heart started doing acrobatics, and I quick turned back around and stared at nothing in the bushes. This was crazy. This was *crazy.* Ugly guys should never drink. It should be against the law. Ugly guys should never never never never never never never never never drink.

"Never," I said, out loud, like that was the end of it. My mind didn't stop, though. My mind went right on thinking about Sheri, like a soldier who goes right on shooting after the war's over. She was pretty drunk. And the way she looked at me a couple of times, it really did look like she was taking me seriously. Plus it was dark in the basement—maybe she forgot who I was, forgot what I looked like, just a little.

My heart was really flopping around now. It was happening too fast. Suddenly we were drunk and suddenly she was looking at me without laughing and asking me questions and suddenly everything was maybe. What should I do? I was so used to *not a chance,* I didn't know what to do with *maybe.* What should I say? What did she want? I wished I'd had everything on videotape so I could watch it all over again, just to be sure. How drunk was I? Was I making it up? It didn't feel like I was making it up. Should I ask her to dance? Should I go back in there and ask her to dance? Should I show her the other letters? Should I let her actually read them, let her know everything?

I couldn't breathe, thinking about Sheri knowing everything. My brain felt crowded with all this stuff, and then, on top of it all, I suddenly remembered Tom. Sheri was Tom's girlfriend. Tom and Sheri were going out. I'd done such a good job forgetting they were going out, now it seemed like a surprise. You're kidding! Tom and Sheri?

I might not have cared if Tom wasn't my brother, if we just weren't siblings. It sounded bad, though, dancing with your brother's girlfriend, kissing your brother's girlfriend. I imagined someone telling me that his little brother kissed his girlfriend when she was drunk at a party. It didn't sound good. It didn't make the little brother sound like someone you could depend on in a plane crash.

Of course, Tom didn't sound like any hero, either, taking credit for those letters even though I wrote them. It sounded pretty sleazy, when I stopped to think about it. Especially since he knew it was the letters that made the difference; it was the letters that made him seem different from anyone she'd ever known. He should've told her. He should've told Sheri I wrote the letters. Somebody should've told her. They wouldn't even have been going out if it hadn't been for me. That counted for something, didn't it? Didn't that make a difference? That the only reason she noticed Tom was because of my letters? How'd she say it? The letters made him seem different from anyone she'd ever known. That was actually me. I was actually the one who was different from anyone she'd ever known.

I took a step toward the door and saw it open, the music from inside spilling out toward me. The door opened halfway, and Sheri slipped out backward and softly closed the door behind her like she was trying not to wake a baby. The door closed on the music pouring out, and Sheri quietly walked along the side of the house toward the dark trees along the street. She was leaving. She didn't even look around to wave good-bye; she was just going away. Why? What was wrong? I started to call out to her, but then remembered I had her car keys. What did she plan on doing? Walk home? Was she going to walk home? That wasn't too safe, some girl walking along the road in the dark. I'd better walk with her. Even if she didn't want me to, I figured I'd better walk her home. Why was she leaving, anyway? Was she going to get sick? Was that it? Was she going to throw up all over the front yard? Why didn't she say something? I could take care of her. I could get her a diet Pepsi to wash the taste out of her mouth. I could wipe her face with a wet towel. I could call a cab and take her home—make sure she got inside all right.

I started to walk toward the front of the house when the basement door opened again and Jay Dannon and Sam Milay fell out, looking like they were trying to tackle each other.

"Hey, lookie who it is," Jay said, pointing at me. Sam didn't hear him, though, because he was staring at Don and Kiel making out. It made me feel less like a sexual deviant, seeing other people stare at Don and Kiel. I didn't know if being drunk made it interesting to watch people make out, or if Don and Kiel were just really good at it.

"What're you doing here, man?" Jay asked, smiling as he walked toward me. I quick stuck my hands in my pockets. "That's pretty low, going to a party after what happened to your sister."

Jay was the schmucky kind of guy who picked on easy targets, like Sonny or even little Herb

Hillgrew. I didn't know what Jay'd seen or what he'd heard about Tracy, but I wasn't going to let him get to me.

"Don't you care about your family?"

"I love to rock and roll. . . ." Sam started singing suddenly, sounding angry, like he was mad Don and Kiel were so good at making out. "Kickin' my very soul."

"Hey, Sam. Sam! I think we've got a deaf-mute here. A regular Helen Keller."

Sam stopped playing air guitar to look. "Hey! It's O'Reilly-head."

I took a step back and looked toward the dark trees at the front of the house. Jay was a schmuck and a coward, but Sam was the type of guy who might just start punching you for the fun of it.

"He doesn't give a shit about his sister," Jay said. "You believe that?"

Sam walked toward me. I'd never noticed he was almost a head taller than I was. "How you doing, O'Reilly-head?"

"Pretty good," I said fast, barely opening my mouth. Sam was smiling a not-happy grin, like he was remembering the time in homeroom when I made fun of his laugh. My heart felt like I was already running.

Jay pointed at me, looking at Sam like he was an attack dog. "You believe that? Coming to a party after what happened to his sister!"

"We're talking rude," Sam said, still moving forward, about to walk through me.

Jay wasn't lying; he wasn't making it up. Sam was too stupid to make-believe. I looked at Jay. "What happened to my sister?" Was she pregnant? In an accident?

"You believe that!" Jay said, still pointing. "Now he's pretending like he doesn't know what happened!"

Sam laughed his idiot-sounding laugh into my face, his breath smelling like beer vomit. I shoved him away.

"What the hell happened?" I said, walking toward Jay, who wasn't any bigger than I was.

He took a step back but kept smiling. "She's in jail, man. She's been arrested."

# Chapter 14

**W**hat're you talking about?" I asked, scared because I knew Jay wasn't lying.

"Drugs," he said.

*"What?"*

A whole vanful of Rukes got arrested for possession and might get charged with trafficking, too. Jay said that Gerald Barney saw everything— the cops dragging the Rukes out of the van and handcuffing them and stuffing them into three or four squad cars. Gerald knew Tracy from orchestra and said she kept screaming at the cops, even after they had her handcuffed.

"How do you—? This—"

I didn't want to believe it, but Gerald Barney wouldn't bullshit. Gerald Barney was a nice guy. He played the flute, for crying out loud. But what was this stuff about *trafficking?* And *screaming?* This was Tracy they were talking about. Tracy wasn't a drug dealer. Tracy wasn't a screamer. What were the cops doing to her? Was she actually *taking* drugs? Was that it? What kind of drugs made you scream at police?

I must've looked like my life had exploded in my face, because Jay was just watching me, smiling. I turned and walked out to the street and started hitchhiking in the dark, the headlights making me squint as they sped by. The road was pretty narrow and it was scary with the cars flying by, but I was so mad at Dad that I felt like it would've served him right if I'd gotten hit. What did I tell him about Tracy? What did I say? I knew Mickey was bad news; I knew he was trouble. All you had to do was look at him. Tracy never should've been hanging around with guys like Mickey. She never should've been dressing like a slut. Now she was in jail. For drugs!

"Maybe now you'll listen," I said out loud, kicking the gravel at the side of the road.

I walked fast, mad at Dad and mad at Tracy and mad that Sheri had to go the other way down the road to walk home. Now I'd never get to talk to her, never get to find out why she skulked away without saying good-bye. I couldn't believe Tracy had to pick *tonight* to get arrested. I couldn't believe I had to hear from Jay Dannon that my sister went to jail for drugs.

"Shit!" I hollered, kicking the ground again, suddenly raging mad at Tracy for screwing up her life like this. She had *talent,* real talent. Even Sonny's sister saw it and wanted Tracy to record some songs with her. Tracy was the only person I'd ever met who was different, who you knew was different as soon as she walked into a room or pulled out her guitar. She was weird—she was definitely weird—but it was genius weird. It was the kind of weird you read about in *People* magazine.

And she'd blown it! *"Son of a——"* I couldn't believe she'd blown it. I squeezed my fists, wanting to punch trees. Why'd she have to do this? Why didn't she just——?

I tried to think of how I could say I planted the drugs on her, how I panicked and dumped the stuff in Tracy's purse. It wouldn't be any big deal for me, getting arrested for drugs. It wouldn't ruin my life; I was just going to go to some below-average college, anyway. It'd probably help my application because they'd think it would increase their student-body diversity, having a convicted criminal in the freshman class.

I stomped down the road, shaking my head that Tracy would do this. After a while I calmed down, though, and started walking on my toes because of the blisters on the heels of my feet. I must've looked like a ballet dancer, and I got mad at the cars that wouldn't stop to pick up one rotten little hitchhiker. What was wrong with these people?

The kitchen light was on as I walked up the driveway. I got right up to the window and looked through the curtains. Matilda was at the stove, and then I saw Dad and Tracy sitting at the table. *Tracy?* What the——? Did they already post bail? How'd they do it so fast? Did Dad put it on Visa?

"Hello," I said, trying to sound offhand and look normal as I came through the door. Matilda was putting steaming cups of something in front of Dad and Tracy. Tracy's hair had dried in wet-looking clumps. "What's going on?" I asked innocently.

Dad was chewing on a couple of toothpicks and glared at Tracy. "Are you going to tell him?"

Tracy reached over and grabbed the saltshaker and twirled it on the tabletop. "I got arrested for making animal sounds."

*"What?"* I looked at Dad. Did he actually *believe* this? Didn't the police tell him about the drugs? About the screaming?

"That's right. *Arrested,*" Dad said, nodding his head at me, misunderstanding why I looked so surprised. "Your little sister was arrested. Hand-cuffed, fingerprinted. Everything."

"What're you talking about, animal sounds?" I couldn't understand why the police would lie to Dad about the drugs. Did Dad think the cops would arrest a whole vanful of Rukes for singing "Old McDonald Had a Farm"?

"Your sister and her friends," Dad said, sitting up, spitting out the words, "thought it would be fun to make snorting pig sounds at the police."

"We didn't think it would be fun! We thought it was ridiculous a jerk cop wanted to arrest Clay for making pig sounds. She wasn't even doing it at him. The whole thing was just stupid."

Dad leaned forward. "Why was Clay making pig sounds in the first place?"

"Look, it doesn't matter. All *right?*" Tracy shot me a look like it was all my fault.

"You got arrested for making pig sounds?" I was almost laughing, and Tracy grabbed the salt-shaker like she was going to make me eat it.

"Do us all a favor and drop dead."

I couldn't believe it. I was so happy, so relieved it wasn't drugs. Mickey wasn't a drug kingpin; Tracy wasn't snorting coke before homeroom. Her life wasn't over. She was still going to be famous and get on talk shows and complain about how one of her older brothers ruined her childhood. It was great news, getting arrested for pig sounds.

"Don't you think it's kind of funny, in a way?" I looked from Dad to Matilda. "I mean, how many people get a criminal record for sounding like a pig? It's almost like—"

"That's enough!" Dad said in his loud voice. I knew I was safe when he used his loud voice.

"You realize how stupid the cops look? Arresting kids for pig sounds."

"You're such a loser," Tracy said.

I stood smiling with my mouth open. "What're you mad at me for? I didn't get you arrested!"

"Capital L. You know what that stands for?"

"Oink, oink. You know what that stands for?"

"Big loser."

"Big pig."

"That's enough." Dad's voice was quiet. We shut up.

The door opened behind me, and I looked over my shoulder. Tom slipped inside, his eyes careening away from us as he turned around to shut the door. All the relief I was feeling about Tracy spilled out in a single wave. Tom. I kept completely forgetting Tom.

"Hi," he said, his back to us as the door clicked shut.

No one said anything at first. Tom's head was down and his shoulders were hunched forward like he was about to curl up into a ball.

"Would you like some hot chocolate?" Matilda asked.

"No, thanks," Tom said, turning mechanically and heading for the doorway to the front hall. "I'm pretty tired. Good night."

We watched as he walked out of the kitchen and listened to his feet clomp up the stairs and into his room. I was afraid Matilda would try to say something *therapeutic,* but luckily she kept her mouth shut. Finally, Dad said we should all go to bed.

I didn't see Tom on Sunday, even though I stuck around all day long thinking Sheri might call about her keys. Matilda brought some food to Tom's room but just left it without trying to talk to him.

Monday he didn't go to school.

Tuesday he went to school, and when I got home, I found him in the den with the television on. He didn't hear me come in, and I just stood there thinking how television was progress; television would at least get his mind off it. Then I looked at the dark screen. He was watching the play. Coach Vincent must've let him borrow the videotape, and Tom was watching Willy shake off the tackler long enough to throw the ball toward the end zone. Then Tom hit the slow-motion button, and the ball slowly jerked through the air, frame by frame, in his direction. You could see his numbers on the back of his jersey. I tiptoed back out again without waiting to watch the ball fall out of his hands and into the mud.

Tracy was in the kitchen, reading. She'd been grounded for two weeks for getting herself arrested. She hadn't even *looked* at me since then, so when I saw her in the kitchen, I snorted some really realistic pig sounds.

"Capital L," she said, not looking up.

"You have the right to remain silent," I told her and added a couple of more snorts. Tracy spent her life more or less ignoring me, but since the arrest, she'd been acting like she'd kill me if she could make it look like a suicide.

Tom had dinner with us Tuesday night, finally, and kept his eyes on his plate the whole time. He looked barely stuck together, like if you bumped into him, an arm or a kneecap might fall off. Tracy was sitting next to him and acted like she was doing life without parole. Then, to cheer things up, Dad announced he was taking everyone out for ice cream.

"I can't," I said.

"Yes, you can."

"I'm on a diet," Tracy told him.

"Tough."

I explained to him about math homework due tomorrow and an English paper and a social studies project and a science lab. I wasn't lying. All that stuff was due, but a lot of it was already late and I'd probably never actually get to it. It didn't matter, anyway. Dad said I could fail for the quarter, but I was going to eat ice cream. I stood by the telephone with my hands in my pockets while everyone got ready.

I still had her keys. I carried them around and kept checking my pocket to make sure they hadn't fallen out. There was the key to her Toyota and three other keys on a wooden key chain that spelled *Sheri*. She had to call eventually. Did she forget handing them to me? Did she forget that whole night? Did she *want* to forget that whole night? Half a million times I thought about calling her, but besides the keys, what would I talk about?

I couldn't even write to her anymore, since the party. I'd sit down and just stare at the paper in front of me. It seemed so pointless. If I was just going to add another letter to the pile in the bottom of my T-shirt drawer, why bother? And if I was going to show it to her . . .

But I couldn't show it to her. She was going out with Tom. What could I say to Tom's girl-friend? What could I say while they were still going out? They were still going out, weren't they? Were they still going out?

I wanted to know. I wanted her to call and tell me, one way or another, and it drove me up a wall having to go on this family outing for ice cream. What if Sheri *did* call? What if she suddenly decided she *did* want to talk to me, and I missed it? What if she called and I wasn't there and then she changed her mind and decided she never wanted to talk to me ever again? It was possible.

When we got home, I checked the messages on the machine. Nothing.

At school sometimes, in health class or maybe while we were supposed to be writing in our English journals, I'd pull Sheri's keys out and look at them. There was a little tiny one that looked like it went to a diary or something, and I'd daydream that she wrote about me in the diary and would carefully make sure every night that it was locked. I'd daydream about her reading it out loud to me sometime—maybe when we were both in college—reading out loud the funny things she had said about me, how she had been confused and hadn't known how she felt about me.

Other times, though, like once when Sonny and I were in the newspaper office and his girlfriend, Laura, dropped by to say hi, I felt all over again that sinking feeling of hearing life rush by in the dark. What Sheri said to me at that party, it could have meant anything. Those looks she gave me—she might've been remembering Christmas when she was a kid, or she might've been trying not to throw up. If it was true, the stuff I hoped, why hadn't she called? I'd shake my head, thinking about it, and feel gripped by an overwhelming sense of life happening somewhere out there. Somewhere out there people were laughing and holding hands and looking at each other. Somewhere out there a bunch of people were sharing a beach house and playing volleyball and toasting marshmallows in a bonfire on the beach. High school was when a lot of life happened—I could hear it happening just listening to Sonny and Laura whisper to each other outside in the hallway. It sucked, knowing there was all this wonderful life going on behind my back while I sat around wondering:

Was she ever going to call?

# *Chapter 15*

**F**riday night, Willy came by and announced he was kidnapping Tom.

"Good luck," Dad told him. Willy went upstairs. Five minutes later, Tom left with him. I sat by the phone in the den, watching the beginning of some foreign film with Dad and Matilda, who were all snuggled up together on the couch. Between the subtitles and Dad and Matilda, though, I couldn't take it, and I went into the kitchen and started reading some book for English. Sonny and Laura and a bunch of people were watching movies over at his house, and they'd invited me to come over, but I didn't want to be away from the phone all night. If Sheri called and Dad or Matilda answered, they'd just tell her Tom was out, and she'd never get a chance to say she was actually calling for me.

Tracy came down to the kitchen for a diet Pepsi and went back upstairs again without saying anything to anybody. She was pouting because she was supposed to go on that art trip to New York in the morning, but Dad had told her grounded meant grounded.

Eventually Dad and Matilda went to bed, and I sat in the quiet, listening to the wind outside and expecting the phone to ring. Was she home? She might not have been home. She might've been out with friends. Drinking, maybe. Was she drinking? Was she getting drunk enough to call?

I couldn't concentrate and went into the den and sprawled out on the couch. I turned on the TV and grabbed a *Newsweek* and stared at photographs and turned pages like I was ready to tear them out and eat them. Out of the corner of my eye I could see the phone sitting there under the lamp. I threw down the *Newsweek* and shut off the lamp and lay down on my side, facing the TV. Sometime after midnight Tom got home, sounding like he was trying to tear off the front door.

"I'm OK, I'm OK," he whispered, slurring his

words. "No, really, I mean it. You've been great, but I'm OK now. Really."

Who was he talking to? A cop? Did he and Willy get pulled over? Arrested? The couch faced away from the front door, so lying down I couldn't see anything.

"I just need to wash my face," Tom said. "I'll be right there." He bumped into something hard and then walked down the hall to the bathroom. Was it Willy's father? His older brother? Did Willy have an older brother? I heard the bathroom door close, and then thought I heard footsteps and quick shut my eyes and let my lips hang loose.

"What're you watching?"

My eyes flew open and my mouth closed. I didn't turn to look. I just lay there, listening to my heart. "Hi," I said, still not turning, still not looking up at her.

"He sounds upset with her," Sheri said.

I had to think before I realized she meant the TV. What was she doing here? How'd she end up driving Tom home? Were they going out again? Were they still going out?

"You think he's really going to shoot?" she asked, still watching the TV. I couldn't believe her voice. I hated hearing it. It sounded so normal, so matter-of-fact. Like nothing had happened.

Like she'd completely forgotten. I wanted to scream at her. Why wasn't she talking to me? Why was she watching the stupid TV?

I sat up, stuck my feet on the floor. Sheri was standing behind the couch, so my back was to her. How could she act like this? Was she trying to pretend it never happened, it was all a dream? She gave me her keys, for crying out loud. Did she forget that? Did she forget her keys were right there in my pocket? I sat, my teeth clenched, feeling time running out. Tom would finish washing his face any second now, and he'd walk Sheri to the door and kiss her good night. And Sheri would leave and never even ask about her keys. She had a new set; it didn't matter. I could hold on to this set forever; she didn't care.

"I'm sorry," she said suddenly, softly, her voice different, gentle. She didn't forget. She wasn't pretending it never happened. She knew; she remembered. My whole insides shifted to make room for how I felt.

"I should've talked to you that night instead of sneaking away, but I didn't trust it."

I didn't move, didn't breathe.

"I felt so many things," she whispered. She was whispering to me! "It's so hard to explain."

Try! Just try!

"I think . . . if you knew . . ."

Knew what? *What?* I tried to swallow.

"I'm sorry, Haley."

Everything stopped.

Did she say *Haley?* Like I was a little boy. Cute little Haley. Is that what she said?

Sheri reached out and rested her hand gently on my shoulder. I pulled away, leaned forward. *Haley.* Did she actually say *Haley?* I closed my eyes, my face burning. All this time . . . How could I even think . . . ? *Haley.* My face was on fire. This was like one of those crazy dreams where I'm running down a hill and actually think I've suddenly realized how to fly. How could I even . . . ? Where was that part of me that was supposed to slap me in the face and scream, *"Wake up, wake up! You're dreaming!"?*

"Haley . . ."

I squeezed my fists tight, my eyes still closed. Why didn't she just run into the kitchen and grab the butcher knife?

"Haley, could you at least look at me?"

Was she kidding? Why would I want to look at her? I'd seen her before. I knew what she looked like.

"The letters were *great,*" she said, like she was trying to cheer me up, console me, prove things weren't *all* bad. I couldn't take it anymore. I jabbed my hand into my pocket, pulled out her keys, and reached back, holding them up without looking. Sheri thought about it for a while and finally took the keys and my hand all at the same time. I took my hand back and sat there with my arms crossed.

"In some ways . . ." Her voice trailed off. I waited for more but knew there wasn't going to be more. *In some ways* . . . That was the closest we were going to get.

The bathroom door opened. Sheri quickly hid the keys away.

"Hey ya, Haley!" Tom sounded surprised, like he'd forgotten I lived there, too. "What're you watching? Would you mind some company?" He was talking too loud, trying to prove he was sober. He and Sheri came over and sat on the couch, Sheri in the middle, between us.

"That's the guy who goes around wanting to kill people," she said, pointing to the TV. "And I think she's a cop."

Her voice was all the way back to normal. It was like she had a switch, could turn it on and off. Now it was off.

"Haley? Haley, where are you going?" Tom sounded confused. "Haley, do you want to watch something else?"

I took the steps three at a time. When I got to my room, I felt dizzy. I couldn't believe she had sat down right next to me like that. Like everything was OK again. I grabbed my ski cap and some money off the dresser, threw open my T-shirt drawer, grabbed all the letters and stuffed them into my back pocket.

Outside in the cold, alone, I was OK. I slipped my arms into my jacket, zipped it up, pulled on my ski cap. I walked into the dark of the garage and grabbed my bike and coasted down the driveway. I didn't ride like a maniac, didn't squeeze the handlebars like I was ready to tear them apart. I just coasted down the driveway and pedaled slowly up the street, practically invisible in the dark, hoping I could make myself disappear.

# Chapter 16

I pedaled along, smooth and easy, figuring I'd ride down to the river and spend the night in Marruke Park. One time when we went for a family picnic out there—back when Dad was still trying to get us used to Matilda—I was crawling around the cliffs looking out over the Potomac and found some rock crevices that were almost caves. I could spend the night in one of them, and then in the morning, maybe I could follow some road that went alongside the river. Maybe follow it out to the ocean and spend the winter at some beach. I could find a cheap place to live and get a part-time job in a local grocery store and spend my days off walking along the shoreline in the cold. I pictured gray, wet, frigid days—no sunshine, no people. Perfect.

My fingers started feeling icy and brittle, sitting naked out there on the handlebars. I wondered what frostbite felt like but kept pedaling away until I was on the other side of Bascom. As soon as I had Bascom behind me, I stopped at an all-night supermarket for a pair of gloves. I only had twenty-three dollars, but I still got the more expensive gloves with the fluffy fake sheepskin inside, because I figured anything was better than a couple of fingers falling off from frostbite. I also bought a loaf of bread, even though I didn't realize how hungry I was until I got outside and ate a slice. Bread never tasted so good. Sitting in the parking lot with my back against a streetlight, I balled up three or four more slices and popped them into my mouth.

I felt great just sitting there, but then I checked the lump I was sitting on and realized it was the letters to Sheri. The letters that had piled up in my T-shirt drawer. I got up and looked around as I walked over to one of the hooded trash cans outside the store. I looked over both shoulders, making sure no one was around, and quick, like I was making a drug deal, slipped the clump of papers into the trash can. Then I stuffed what was left of the bread inside my jacket and rode out of the parking lot.

The bike felt great, just pedaling along at an even, steady pace, but I couldn't push Sheri out of my mind. Had I really thought she might . . . ? What a joke! I shook my head and closed my eyes for two, three, four seconds, almost hoping a bus would jump out and land on top of me. I wished I could erase it all or take a razor blade and scrape it away.

I was worse than Dad. Dad had crazy dreams, but at least they were *nice* dreams. His dreams just involved Mr. Bruce Springsteen playing his music and everyone living happily ever after. I had dreams about Sheri falling in love with me and dumping Tom, dreams about Matilda dying and Dad moving us back to New York and getting back together with Mom. My dreams involved people getting hurt or killed.

A sheet of newspaper flew up at me from between two parked cars, and I nearly fell over trying to dodge it. If God wanted to get me, though, I knew he'd get me. If it wasn't a dog chewing me up, it'd be a car crushing me against a wall, and if it wasn't a car, it'd be one of those crazies you read about in the paper who get a thrill out of watching people bleed. I felt like something was going to happen; I wasn't going to just get away with all this stuff. I almost *wanted* something to happen, like that was the only way things could be OK again.

I stopped at a gas station—a real gas station, with a garage and an office instead of some guy locked up in a glass booth—and bought a Milky Way and looked at a couple of maps. Right away it was clear that following the river out to the ocean wasn't going to work because the Potomac didn't even go to the ocean. It emptied into the Chesapeake Bay, and even getting to *that* looked like a real pain in the ass. The main problem was the river didn't have a nice, normal, even shoreline but kept jutting in and out in all sorts of weird ways. I started wondering if I could rent a canoe or maybe find a raft somewhere and drift downstream. I liked the idea of just drifting along, watching the shore go by.

After buying one of the maps and a thin little flashlight, I had a measly fourteen dollars left. I climbed back onto my bike. It wasn't much of a ride from there to Marruke Park, which was a lot darker than I'd thought it'd be. I listened to the leafless tree branches overhead, knocking in the wind. What time was it, anyway? How late did the Rukes hang out?

The road ended at a parking lot, and I walked my bike from there—it was safer to step into a ditch than ride into one. Even after my eyes adjusted, all I could see was the night sky through the black branches. I got pretty good at staying on the path, though, because I could feel when I was slanting to one side or the other.

I made it to the lookout point on the cliffs. There was more light there, with the trees gone and the open space. It was windier, too, though, and colder. Every so often a gust came along and seemed like it was trying to pull the bicycle away from me. The rocks looked a lot more dangerous in the dark, and way down below I could hear the river pounding. Now what? I tried my little flashlight, but any light it threw seemed to get sucked up like the darkness was just a big sponge. I squinted at the rocks, trying to think. I didn't want to die. I didn't want my brains spilling out on some rock sixty feet below.

For the first time since I'd left, I started wondering what I was actually going to do. I started doubting the beach idea. It reminded me of when I was a little kid and got mad at Mom and

Dad and swore I'd never talk to them again. I believed it, too. I really believed they could do anything—they could pull my eyeballs out—and I still wouldn't talk to them. But then, two hours later, I'd be politely asking for another piece of cake.

I stood there, listening to the water down below, mad at myself for not wanting to die. Would I even make it through the night? Would I even find someplace else to sleep? Or would I just ride home and slither into my own warm little bed?

Back out on the road, I took some wrong turns on purpose, hoping to get lost. It worked pretty well, actually, and I got to a 7-Eleven I didn't think I'd ever seen before. I bought a Coke that tasted cold and delicious, and I walked outside and looked up at the stars, feeling strong and clean and alive. This was life. I'd never thought about standing outside a 7-Eleven as life before, but it was. This was living. I got goose bumps. I was standing outside a 7-Eleven at three o'clock in the morning on a dark, perfectly still street, looking up at the stars. I was lost, I was going to stay out all night.

I was alive. Me. Hale O'Reilly.

I took a good look around: up and down the

road; across the street at a flower store; back at the stars. I thought it was weird when we first moved down to Washington that these were the same stars they had up in New York; that Kevin and Jimmy could be looking up at the same stars I saw, that even Allison May could be looking at the same stars I was looking at. I sipped some Coke and wondered how Allison May was doing, how Kevin and Jimmy were doing, if they ever wrote our screenplay. And even though I kept watching the stars and kept drinking the Coke, I could feel the happy alive feeling slipping away, pulling back. This was OK, standing here with the stars, but it wasn't New York. Staying out all night was OK, but it wasn't Kevin and Jimmy. I finished off the Coke and then stopped, suddenly realizing: I could see them. I could see Kevin and Jimmy. I could go to New York.

Now. Tomorrow.

I threw the Coke bottle away and jumped back on my bike. I could go in place of Tracy on the art trip to New York. She'd already paid, but she'd been grounded. All I had to do was show up. Tracy could be a guy's name, and they wouldn't be expecting someone to sneak on using someone else's name, anyway. The bus left at six.

I could make it, no problem. I started to ride away.

Except I didn't know where I was. I jumped off my bike and ran into the 7-Eleven, scaring the guy behind the counter because I must've looked like I was in a hurry to blow his head off. I asked him how to get to Oakdale, but he was Vietnamese and didn't act like he'd had a lot of people asking him how to get to Oakdale. I pulled out my map and asked him, "Where? Where?" He stared at the map while I looked at the clock, hearing tick-tick-tick going off in my head.

The map wasn't helping—It occurred to me, how much would a Vietnamese map help *me?*— So I asked what was the name of the road outside. "Oyster," he said; or that's what I heard, anyway, but I didn't see any *Oyster* on the map.

"Oh! OK!" I said, making a big deal like I'd found it. The guy looked happy, and I thanked him and jogged out. About a quarter of a mile up the road I found an intersection—Orsten and Marifield. The flashlight worked great now, when I held it two or three inches away from the map.

"Holy—" I swallowed, holding my finger on Orsten and Marifield and looking all the way up at Oakdale. It had to be I-didn't-know-how-many miles, but a lot. I planned a route and jumped back on my bike and took off, still hearing the tick-tick-tick like my head was a bomb. I pictured walking into the McDonald's on Broadway and seeing Kevin and Jimmy in there and just sitting down next to them like nothing had happened. Kevin would stare at me with his mouth open and Jimmy would keep saying it was unfreakingbelievable until we told him to shut up.

I got lost, somehow, at the first turn and had to backtrack. It's a lot more fun to get lost when you want to. I stopped to look at the map again and then took off. Tick-tick-tick. I liked the idea of running out of time, of beating the clock. I could do it, I knew I could do it—until the bike chain fell off on Lee Highway.

I'd downshifted and was pedaling hard up a hill and didn't realize what was going on until the chain was wedged tight between the gear sprocket and the frame. I pushed the bike up to the next streetlight and tried to jiggle the chain free. Then I grabbed it and yanked and got both hands covered with grease. In a trash can I found an old shoe that was bent up at the toe like the foot had snapped off. I tried using the shoe like a crowbar, to pry the chain free, but the only thing that moved was the loopety-loop thing below the gears on the back wheel. I cursed and then stood up and cursed some more. Then I imagined the toes still sitting there in the shoe, and I threw it back at the trash can and made a basket without even trying.

A cold breeze swept down the hill. I couldn't even put the gloves on now because of the grease on my hands. My eyes were itchy, and I just wanted to go to sleep. Or even sit down. I thought about sitting down and resting my eyes for a second, but I didn't know what time it was and started pushing my bike up the hill.

At the top of the hill I found a pay phone and called for a cab, but the guy wanted a credit-card number. I told him I was sixteen; I didn't have a credit card. He said they didn't pick up minors and hung up.

What is it with people?

I coasted down the other side of the hill and then jogged along a flat area. The color of the sky was shifting from black to dark blue. I knew where I was and tried to calculate how far it was to school, but I was so tired, I couldn't even picture how long the streets were. I felt like if I leaned just enough against the bike, I could sleep and jog at the same time. I'd never been up all night before, and I had to squint just to keep my eyes open.

I made up a little song to stay awake. "What—time—is—it? What—time—is—it? Whaaaat—tiiiime—is it?"

The song got boring real fast, though, and I just jogged along and fantasized about sleeping—stretching my legs out in between cool sheets, dropping the side of my head against my pillow. That was the life; that was real living. Who cared about a stupid bus ride to New York?

I jogged up the last little hill to school and saw it. Bus. There it was. Bus. Parked under a streetlight in front of school. But no people. Was I early? No people anywhere. Then I realized—they were on the bus! Everybody was on the bus, and the bus was pulling away. Shit! I ran full speed, waving my free hand, my jacket unzipped and flying behind me. The bus stopped. I caught up to it just as Mr. Wilson climbed off, his pregnant-looking belly bouncing up from the last step.

"Who are you?"

"O'Reilly," I said, between gasping breaths.

"Huh? What's that?" He checked his clipboard. "You're not O'Reilly. O'Reilly's a girl. Someone just finished telling me she wasn't coming."

I told him I was Tracy's brother and that I

was going in her place. "My dad checked it with Mr. Blackburn. He said it was OK."

"Huh? What's that? Blackburn? Mr. Blackburn approved it?"

Was he on the bus? "I think it was Blackburn."

"I'm surprised Mr. Blackburn would approve something like this without checking with me first."

"I could've sworn Dad said Mr. Blackburn."

"Huh?" Mr. Wilson looked at me with his tongue stuck in his cheek, trying to think. He was an assistant principal—he only dealt with kids who lied to him. "Hold it right there," he said, and climbed back on the bus.

I went over and casually locked up my bike like nothing was wrong. When I turned around, Wilson's belly was bouncing off the bus again. And then Clay jumped off right after him. Her body went stiff when she saw me. Wilson stood sideways between us, like a referee.

"Didn't you tell me Tracy O'Reilly wasn't coming?" he asked Clay.

"So?" she said. Typical Ruke attitude.

"Did she tell you anything about her brother taking her place?"

"She wouldn't know about it," I said quick. "My dad just called like yesterday."

"Huh? What's that? Yesterday?" Wilson sounded like he'd caught me.

"Pretty sure it was yesterday."

Wilson pointed at Clay and talked faster now, like he was winning. "And you talked to Tracy last night. Isn't that what you told me?"

What. Did Clay give him her life's story?

"Yeah, I talked to her," Clay said, and looked past him at me. Looked at me like I was going to rot in hell.

"Did she say anything about her brother taking her place?"

Clay kept looking at me, her mouth shut.

"What's that?" Wilson said. "Did she say anything about her brother?"

Clay looked at him. "Yeah," she said, sounding angry, like she resented being bothered.

I thanked her twice, following her down the aisle on the bus. She flopped down in the last row on the bathroom side, and there was an empty seat next to her, so I sat there and thanked her again.

"Nice hands," Clay said, looking at them.

The interior lights were on, and the black grease on my hands made me look like I'd spent the night carrying around car engines. I went back to the bathroom and washed my hands three times and looked at myself in the mirror. It was worse than usual—my hair sticking up in a permanent windblown look from riding my bike all night and dark puffy blotches under my eyes. I looked uglier, but older, too.

I sat back down next to Clay. She was wearing a black shirt with a collar that went high up on the sides.

"You look nice," I said.

Clay turned her head. "You look like crap."

"No kidding." I laughed without knowing what was funny and closed my eyes and rested my head against the palm of my hand.

"You want the window?"

I was already half-asleep and for a second thought it was part of a dream, but then I recognized Clay's voice and opened my eyes.

"If you're going to sleep," she said, "you might as well have something to lean against."

I just looked at her for a second. "Oh. Thanks."

We both stood up to switch places, and I got a whiff of her perfume or shampoo or something. It reminded me of the night of the game, in the rain, when I hurt Clay's feelings and her face looked like the face of a girl.

I went to sleep remembering that face.

# Chapter 17

ey. We're here. Hey!" Someone shook my arm, and I woke up enough to hear the steady rumble of the bus. "Hey," Clay said. I opened my eyes and saw, inches from the window, a shiny wall streaking by.

"What," I said, moving my head away.

"We're in the Lincoln Tunnel."

*"What?"* I sat up. It looked like a tunnel. It was definitely a tunnel. "Wait. Are you sure this isn't Baltimore?"

"You think I'm a moron? You've been asleep for five-and-a-half hours."

I looked at Clay, suspicious. It didn't feel like

five and a half hours, but why would she lie about it? I watched her brushing her hair. It'd never occurred to me that Rukes brushed their hair. Clay saw me watching and held out the brush.

"You want to borrow it?"

I automatically reached up with one hand to touch my hair, which felt stiff, like a cheap wig. Sometimes when I woke up groggy I forgot all about being ugly. I looked out the window just as we came out of the tunnel into Manhattan. The sky was dark and overcast, which cheered me up. I loved New York in the rain, and I got excited about being home.

"Where were you last night?" Clay asked.

"I went bike riding."

"All night?"

"I couldn't sleep."

"You did all right on the way up."

"Mmm." I yawned, looking out the window, just like a tourist. We stopped for a light on Eighth Avenue, and a couple of Spanish guys sitting on a stoop looked at us. I remembered what I used to think of tour buses, and it felt weird being on one. The streets were dirtier than they were in Washington, but there was more going on, you could tell.

"Now what're you going to do?" Clay asked. "Go see your old friends?"

"I'll probably give them a call, yeah." I couldn't wait to see Kevin and Jimmy. It woke me up, just thinking about it. "How about you? Are you going to the museum?"

"Yeah, that ought to be fun for about twelve minutes."

"Museums should have video games."

Clay snorted. "Steal the Masterpiece."

I acted like I was reading promotional material. " 'In which experts teach you how to steal real paintings.' "

We figured the first stage of the game would involve killing the guards quietly and disposing of the bodies without leaving trails of blood. Clay even laughed a real laugh once—no snorting. Suddenly we were on Madison Avenue, making a turn onto Eighty-fourth, a block from the museum.

"So you have any great ideas on where to go besides the museum?" Clay asked.

"I don't know. There's Central Park."

*"Oooh.* That sounds like barrels of fun."

"There's Bloomingdale's."

"You used to go to *Bloomingdale's?*"

Kevin and Jimmy and I used to stand outside Bloomingdale's and watch the women go in and come out. I doubted it would have the same appeal for Clay.

"How 'bout F. A. O. Schwarz? That's a big toy store."

Clay's eyes lit up. "You think they'll let me play with the dollies?"

"Sorry. I didn't know you were so mature."

"I didn't come to New York to go to a toy store."

"Then take a subway down to Wall Street and pretend you're a corporate executive! I don't know what you want to do."

Clay looked out the windows on the other side of the bus. Why was she being such a jerk all of a sudden? Was she one of those Dr.-Jekyll-and-Mr.-Hyde people if she didn't take drugs to keep her normal? We read about people like that in health class. Had Clay forgotten her morning medication?

The bus pulled up in front of the museum, and I tried to push my hair down on my head. Clay had put her brush in her backpack, and I was afraid that if I asked to borrow it, she'd go off the deep end. What was her problem, anyway? She was all right when she wasn't a jerk. She actually had a sense of humor.

"You want to come with me?" I asked, fast,

before I thought about it too long and realized it was a stupid thing to do.

Clay turned her head, looking annoyed. "What?"

"It was just an idea." My face was on fire. "I'm sorry. I wasn't—I just thought if you had nothing to do. . . ."

"What did you say?"

I shook my head. "I didn't say anything! I'm sorry. Forget it." What was I thinking? Was I crazy?

"I didn't hear you!" Clay said, enunciating her words like I was deaf and she wanted me to lip-read. "You were mumbling. Will you quit being a pain in the ass and kindly tell me what you said?"

I exhaled. Was I getting set up? Was she going to scream out so the whole bus could hear, "You want me to do *what?*" I looked out the window at the museum. "I was just asking if you wanted to come meet my friends."

"Sure," Clay said.

I looked at her. "Are you serious?"

"Are you?"

I could feel myself strutting, walking into the museum. I had friends. The rest of these kids were tourists, but I had places to go, friends to see. I knew that part of the reason I asked Clay along was to show off: show off Kevin and Jimmy, show off that I had had pretty cool friends when I lived in New York. I felt different, confident—like my old self again. Maybe Dad was right, maybe I *was* getting a little weird down there in Virginia. I felt OK now, though. I felt like it was all coming back again, like anything could happen.

We found the pay phones downstairs. I knew both numbers by heart and called Kevin first, looking at Clay while it rang. She was wearing her heavy-duty combat boots, and her black hair had a maroon tinge to it that I'd never noticed before. I hadn't thought about it when I asked her along, but right away Kevin and Jimmy were going to think she was my girlfriend. Especially Jimmy. Neither of us had ever had a girlfriend, but Jimmy was always telling me about these girls who liked me.

"I saw her looking at you," he'd tell me. "I swear to God."

Even with the combat boots and the maroon hair, I actually didn't mind the idea of Kevin and Jimmy thinking Clay was my girlfriend, except it was going to be depressing telling them the truth.

Mrs. Pearson answered the phone, and I asked

for Kevin. He was going to be so surprised, I couldn't wait to talk to him.

"Hello?"

"Hey, scumbag!"

Clay gave me a look.

"Hale?" Kevin said. "Is that you?" He sounded like I'd come back from the dead.

"So what the hell's going on?"

"Nothing. Why? What do you mean?"

"I thought you'd still be sleeping."

It seemed like Kevin didn't know what to think. "Where are you?"

I told him about the field trip to the museum. "I came up with a friend," I said, looking at the lines on the floor instead of at Clay. "So, hey, want to meet me at McDonald's?"

"I can't," Kevin said. "I've got to get my hair cut."

Kevin was always clowning around. "Yeah, right."

He said he was serious, that he was going to a semiformal that night and had all sorts of things he needed to get done beforehand. I kept expecting him to laugh. He kept going on and on, but I just stood there waiting for a punch line.

"Maybe we can do something next time you come up," he said, still not laughing. Did he mean it? Was he really not going to meet me at McDonald's? Because he had to go get his *hair* cut?

"Good talking to you, Hale."

"Yeah," I said, and held the phone to my ear, just in case. I hadn't given him the number, so it wasn't like he could call back and say he was kidding. I listened to a couple of clicks and then got a dial tone.

"What's wrong?" Clay asked.

"What." I hung up the phone.

"Are you meeting him?"

"Probably not. I don't think so. He's really busy because of all this stuff he has to do."

"Too busy to see an old friend? Sounds like a jerk."

"What. No. He's just a really busy guy. I should've called first to let him know I was coming." I was already dialing Jimmy's number, hoping Clay would get off my back.

"Hello?"

"Jimmy, how you doin'? This is Hale."

"Holy moly. Hale?"

I started feeling better. "How you doin'?"

"Hale who?"

"What a riot," I said, but laughed anyway.

"Holy moly. Hale. Where are you? This is

unfreakingbelievable. Are you still down in what-chamacallit? Tennessee? Alabama?"

"You want to go to McDonald's?"

"Are you here? Are you serious? Are you really here? Holy moly. They let you out?" He sounded blown-away surprised—exactly how I'd thought Kevin was going to react.

"Hey, what's the deal with Kevin?"

"What do you mean? Did you talk to him? What'd he say? Did he say anything?"

"About what?"

"He didn't say anything?" Jimmy was great at stringing you along.

"What are you talking about?"

"Holy moly. I can't believe he didn't say anything to you."

"About the semiformal? Is that what you're talking about?"

"That's all he said? He didn't say anything else?"

"Jimmy—" I let it go. The best thing you could do with Jimmy was try to pretend you didn't care. We said we'd meet at McDonald's in a half hour. I hung up and turned and saw Clay standing there. She saw the shock on my face.

"You want to go alone?" she asked.

"What. No."

"I'd rather stay here, anyway. I have this book I was reading, and I wanted to see some stuff by this Botticelli guy. Is it OK if I don't go?"

I had to talk her into going to McDonald's. Halfway through arguing about it, I started believing what I was saying. I really did want Clay to go with me.

We walked through Central Park toward the West Side. The leaves were gone and everything looked dead. I kept wondering why Kevin had sounded so distant. Did something awful happen? Did he lose a leg in a car accident? Why wouldn't Jimmy tell me?

"Looks like snow," Clay said, watching the sky.

"Too warm," I said. "It'll rain."

"Bet you a condom." Clay held out her hand to shake on it.

"What?"

Clay said she and Tracy always bet condoms. The loser had to go into the guidance office and get a free condom from the basket on the secretary's desk.

"Of course, the secretary has to be sitting there or it doesn't count."

207

"What do you do with them?"

Clay looked at me. "Why? What do *you* do with them?"

"I don't get them."

"Don't give me that. I've seen you grab fistfuls."

"What are you talking about? When?"

"Next time I'll take pictures."

"Yeah, right," I said.

"You're telling me you've never seen a condom?"

"I've seen one. So what?" I didn't know why I was nervous.

"Did you open the package?"

"Maybe."

Clay moved closer. "What'd you do with it?"

"I didn't do *anything* with it."

"You didn't try it on?"

"What are you talking about?" I asked, looking away.

"Tell me you didn't try it on."

I started to laugh.

"I know how guys work."

"No, you don't."

"I see the way guys look at girls. I know what you're thinking."

I shook my head. "This is what kills me about

girls. You have no *idea* what guys are thinking. Or who they think about, or how much they think about them. I mean, you really have no idea." We were crossing the Great Lawn—a wide-open space with a castle at one end, sitting on a cliff, and a view of the buildings far away, surrounding the park.

"Who do you think about?" Clay asked.

I shrugged. "I don't count."

"Why not?"

"Because I don't think anymore."

"Ever? What happened? Have you had an operation?"

"Sort of, yeah."

"And you never ever think about anyone? At all?"

I shrugged, not looking at Clay, afraid she could tell. I didn't even understand how it had started. Was it how nice she was this morning, giving me the window seat? Was it the smell of her shampoo? Or was it going back all the way to the football game, when she stood there in the rain and looked like a human being? It didn't make sense that I'd think about Clay. She was a Ruke. She was *weird*—legitimately weird—and I always tried to ignore weird people as much as possible. But Clay was beyond weird. She was nice. Not nice the way everyone's nice—not nice just when it's easy to be nice. Clay was nice when she *hated* me. Not telling Tracy things she could've told her, not telling Mr. Wilson I was lying. Clay did it when she thought I was a schmuck. Who would do that? Who would be that kind?

"Does that mean you're a pervert?" Clay asked. "If you don't think about people, do you think about cows? Or furniture? Is that it? Do you fantasize about furniture?"

I looked at Clay. She was almost pretty, but she was so *weird!*

"Be honest. Are you infatuated with furniture?"

I looked at her eyes, thinking how I legitimately liked this girl. I liked a *Ruke*. "I'm in love with a lounge chair," I told her.

# Chapter 18

Jimmy'd be late. I warned Clay when we got there. Jimmy was always late.

Clay tapped on the table. "Hey. Why're you so nervous?"

"What. I'm just looking at the door," I said, and took a deep breath to relax. I was worried about letting Jimmy know as fast as I could that Clay and I weren't together, weren't a thing. He'd resent me having a girlfriend. One thing Jimmy and I had in common was not being great-looking. Girls basically acted like we weren't really there, and Jimmy was always telling me about how guys got so stupid about girls and talking to girls and having girlfriends. It just bugged him, being not so great-looking, and it got worse when Kevin started going out with Bernadette Myers. Jimmy wouldn't stop talking about the birthmark on the back of Bernadette's neck and the goofy way she tied back her hair and how in math class she never figured out base five. He was pretty funny about Bernadette, actually, but I didn't want him to start picking on Clay just because he thought we were going out. Clay was so weird she'd be an easy target for him. Jimmy'd ask her about her maroon hair or her shaved eyebrows and act like *he* was thinking about getting some maroon hair and shaving *his* eyebrows. He could make people look really stupid when he wanted to.

"What're you thinking about?" Clay asked.

"Noth—" I stopped, looking past her and seeing Jimmy at the door. I waved, and Clay looked over her shoulder as he walked toward us.

"He's cute," she said.

"Yeah, right." I stood up. Jimmy did look pretty good, actually. He'd gotten taller and his body had filled out in his arms and shoulders.

"Yo, asshole."

"Hey, scumbag."

We shook hands. It felt weird; it might've actually been the first time Jimmy and I shook hands. He looked down at Clay sitting there, staring blankly, like she was riding a crowded subway.

"Oh, Jimmy. This is Clay."

"Hi," he said.

"Clay's like just a friend," I said, and cringed. It didn't sound right.

"Sure," Jimmy said, sitting down next to her, "that's what they all say." He looked at Clay and actually winked at her. Not what you want to do to a Ruke.

"No, really," I said. "Clay doesn't—We're not—" My face was on fire, I was so embarrassed. I looked at Clay. "Aren't we just friends?"

"Not even," she said, looking at Jimmy. "We sat down together on the bus by accident."

I looked at Clay, but she just kept looking at Jimmy. Was she angry? Did she want Jimmy to think we were going out? Even if we *were* going out, I would've thought she wouldn't want people to know it.

Jimmy talked to her about where she came from and what Texas was like and how, instead of going to the Statue of Liberty, tourists should take the Staten Island Ferry. It started getting on my nerves how he kept making small talk when we hadn't seen each other for a year and a half. Eventually, Clay stood up to get herself some coffee and asked Jimmy if he wanted anything. Me she didn't even look at.

"So how's whatchamacallit?" Jimmy asked once she was gone. "Nebraska."

I was watching Clay walk over to the counter, hoping she might look back. "What? Oh, it's OK," I said.

"I can't believe you're here," Jimmy said, shaking his head. "This is unfreakingbelievable."

"So tell me what the deal is with Kevin."

Jimmy looked up quick, like he was nervous, and then tried to hide it by casually flipping his palms up. "I don't know. We don't hang around much anymore."

"What do you mean? Why not?"

Jimmy shrugged and wouldn't look at me. "He hangs around a lot with Bill Moore and those guys."

My mouth dropped open. "Wait a second. Bill Moore?" Bill Moore threw keg parties. Bill Moore played rugby with college guys. "Since when does Kevin hang out with Bill Moore?"

Jimmy looked at me and then moved his eyes away fast, like a criminal. "Since he started seeing Allison May."

I sat, not moving. Jimmy loved sensational news. He was always telling me about bizarre murders and gory accidents where body parts would get lost and end up in pickle jars.

"They started going out last spring. Supposedly they cheat together in chemistry."

This was *Kevin* we were talking about? Kevin Pearson? My friend, Kevin Pearson? Who knew I was stupid about Allison May? Who knew I was madly in love with Allison May? Kevin Pearson was now going *out* with Allison May? Kevin Pearson would do that to a friend?

"He said they wrote you a letter once, but they never mailed it."

"*They* wrote a letter?" My voice was tight like I was about to throw a chair or something. "What do you mean, *they* wrote a letter?"

Jimmy shrugged. "Allison said you asked her out once."

It was like he'd punched me, like he'd nailed me a hard one I didn't know was coming. "She told you that?"

"She told Kevin."

"And that's what the letter was about? About me asking her out?"

"Something like that. All he said was, they were up in her room and her parents were gone."

I imagined Kevin and Allison huddled together in her room, writing the letter. I imagined them slapping their knees and falling over, laughing, holding their sides, laughing and laughing and laughing. I could feel everything tighten up inside and turn hard and cold.

Clay came back with the coffee—one for her and one for Jimmy. I stood up, not looking at anything, and walked away. Got into the bathroom and locked the door. It smelled like a sewer fumigated with a toxic disinfectant. I tried not to breathe and looked at myself in the mirror. It was cracked, so my head was disjointed, my eyes crooked, different skull pieces out of whack. I didn't understand. I didn't get why Allison would tell Kevin I asked her out. Or why Kevin would tell Jimmy. Or why Jimmy would tell me.

"Shit," I said, thinking about Kevin and then Jimmy and then Allison. *"Shit!"* I breathed deeply a couple of times to calm down, and then felt the cold anger fill me up inside. I could hear them laughing. I could've described just what it sounded like, the laughing—Kevin and Allison laughing— and I felt charged up, thinking about it.

I felt an icy electric charge, thinking about the laughing. Everything was flat and calm. It was OK. It was fine. No problem.

When I got back to the table, Clay and Jimmy

nobody was around trying to break in. Dad was a big one for trying to talk to me, for trying to crack open the icy, dull glow. Sometimes I went for long bike rides just to get away from him.

A gust of cold air threw itself at me when I opened the door. For a second I thought there were pieces of ash floating in the air, but actually it was scattered snowflakes drifting by on their own. Clay had been right. I owed her a condom.

The light was against me crossing Broadway, so I headed downtown. Maybe I'd go watch the skaters at Rockefeller Center. It made me feel sad in a good way, watching the skaters and looking up at the huge Christmas tree. There were always some incredible skaters, and there were always couples holding hands like maybe this was their first date together, and they couldn't get over how lucky they were. I was glad for them. It never bothered me, standing there alone, watching all the couples skating, sliding slowly along. It's easier watching happy people when you don't know them.

Clay caught up with me a block and a half down and just walked along beside me, catching her breath. I was surprised at how glad I was to see her, and I wouldn't look at her because I didn't want it to show. I would've given her a flower, though, if I'd had one, or a greeting card or even a Cracker Jack prize.

"He told me about Kevin," she said. Great. Just what I needed, some girl tracking me down to give me sympathy. I took back the flower I would have given her and looked up at the snow. There were enough flakes now to look like the real thing.

"I'm sorry," Clay said.

"About what? What're you sorry about? That Kevin's a schmuck? Big deal. Kevin's a schmuck. So what? Jimmy's a schmuck, too."

"Why is Jimmy a schmuck?"

"No, you're right. Jimmy's not a schmuck. He's a wonderful guy. He's a riot. He should have his own comedy hour." The light was green to cross Broadway, and I quick turned and cut over, thinking maybe I'd just head back to the museum. I didn't feel like watching the skaters, anyway.

When I got to the other corner, someone shoved me from behind with two hands. I wasn't expecting it and went stumbling forward about ten yards, panic in my heart because someone must've thought I was someone else, and if they wanted to kill me, how was I going to prove they had the wrong guy? I turned back and saw Clay standing at the edge of the curb. I had no idea she could push that hard.

*"How stupid ARE you?"* she screamed across at me, and the people walking between us stared at her and then at me. The whole time I grew up, I never remembered getting stared at. You really have to do something in New York to get stared at.

"What are you talking about?"

"Don't you *see?* Are you BLIND?" Clay turned and nearly walked into the front grille of a yellow taxi racing across town, blaring its horn.

"Shit," I said, watching it. Clay kept going. "Will you stop? Clay. *Clay.*"

She was walking fast and it took me half a block to catch up. I had absolutely no idea what she was talking about, except maybe—unless— oh, come on. Was I crazy?

"Will you tell me what the hell you're talking about?" I asked as I caught up. Clay was crying. It was so incredible that for half a second I thought snowflakes were melting on her cheeks, but there were trails coming from her eyes—they were tears. My voice dropped down and turned soft. "Clay. What—?" But what was I going to ask? She was crying. Tears and everything. I couldn't believe it. "Clay—" I had no idea how to do this and finally just jumped in front of her. Clay stopped and looked at me, the tears still along the sides of her nose. My heart was thumping.

"I was jealous. OK?"

Clay brushed the back of her hand across a cheek. "Of what?" she asked, sounding pouty and not looking at me.

"Of you laughing like an idiot at Jimmy's jokes."

Clay crossed her arms and looked down at my sneakers. "What does that matter?"

"You never laugh like an idiot at *my* jokes."

Clay finally looked at me. "So what do you care?"

My heart was flying now. "I care. OK?"

"Why?"

"Because."

"Because why?"

"Look," I said, and stuck my hands in my pockets. "It doesn't matter. All right?"

"How do *you* know?"

"I just know. All right?" I was getting fidgety with Clay looking at me. I hated people looking at me, and I turned my head and saw our reflections in the dark plate-glass window of a fancy-looking restaurant.

"Tell me why you were jealous," Clay said.

I couldn't see my face in the window, but I

could see Clay's silhouette, so I knew she was still looking at me.

"I like you," I said, still watching her silhouette.

"Could you be a little more specific?"

*"What?"* I said, turning to look at her.

"Well, my mother and father like me, too. Do you like me the way they like me?"

What did she want me to say? I put my hands on my hips and stared at her. "No."

Clay stared back. "Well, I don't like you the way your parents do, either," she said, and made a little smile as she walked around me on her way downtown. I stood there and blinked.

# Chapter 19

1 dragged Clay into F. A. O. Schwarz, and we played laser space guns, killing each other over and over again. Then we went by Godiva Chocolates, and Clay wanted to buy a little red sampler for her parents, which made me almost laugh because Clay did not look like the type who would go around buying chocolates to take home to her parents. I actually almost bought Clay some chocolates, too, but I didn't want her thinking I was *assuming* anything. Surprising a girl with a box of chocolates can be really romantic, but not if she doesn't *want* romantic, not if she doesn't

want *your* chocolates. I didn't want Clay thinking I had my hopes up.

I looked out at the snow coming down in big flakes and sticking to everything. It was amazing to me, this whole day. I couldn't believe that I liked a Ruke. That we were walking around New York together, playing space guns and pretending we didn't speak English when salespeople tried to kick us out.

The only thing was, I would've felt better if I knew how Clay felt, one way or the other. Actually, that wasn't true, I realized, as I waited for her to get through the line to buy the little red box. I didn't want to know, one way or the other; if Clay just liked me as a friend, I wasn't in any hurry to hear about it. She could send me a postcard about it later, as far as I was concerned.

It felt hot in the store, all of a sudden, and I told Clay I'd wait outside. I stood on the curb by a No Parking sign, looking in at Clay through the gaps of people walking by along the sidewalk. The snow muffled the sound of everything, so even trucks driving by or horns honking sounded soft and dreamy. It was pretty romantic, actually, looking in at Clay through the people and the snow-flakes.

The problem, though, was looks. *My* looks. Everything came down to looks. I thought about it with that same icy calm I had felt back in McDonald's. The difference between friends and more-than-friends was looks. A pretty face. Looks. Period.

Clay came out of the store, her cheeks bright red, and we went down to see the Christmas tree. We stood there together for a long time, leaning against the railing, watching the skaters. I liked being there alone, but it was a lot more fun with Clay, even though we didn't say anything. I felt like I could just watch the skaters without having to keep her entertained. Eventually I could feel Clay looking at me, and I looked back.

"What?"

"You're awfully paranoid," she said. "You know that?"

"Yeah."

Clay kept looking at me. "Turn around for a second."

"What."

"Just turn around for a second," she said, and grabbed my shoulders and twisted me until I had my back to her. "Yeah, that's it. Stay right there."

I had no idea what was going on until I felt

226

a *pop* on the back of my head and the snow falling down under my collar before I had a chance to wipe it away. By the time I turned around, Clay had another snowball in her hand and threw it at point-blank range but missed. I got her back pretty good when we headed uptown. The streets were slushy and my sneakers got squishy waterlogged, but I still had the gloves I bought the night before, so I could keep firing away. At Fifty-ninth Street, Clay finally called a truce, and we cut over into the park, which was all white and perfect-looking.

"It's like magic," I said, looking up at the snow on the tree branches.

"Oh, *barf,*" Clay said, and scooped up some slush and slung it at me. It hit me like shotgun spray all over my face, and Clay took off running, cutting across a small field between the path and the road. I got over the shock in a hurry and ran after her and caught up pretty quickly, but the wet grass under the snow was slippery, so when Clay dodged out of the way, I almost went flying on by. I threw an arm out at her, though, and quick grabbed on with my other hand, and when my feet went out from under me, I held on. I landed—*thunk!*—on my side, a little twisted, and then—*crunk!*—Clay landed on top of me, our heads knocking together, sounding like coconuts. I was scared for Clay, but after a half-second of shock, she started to laugh.

"Are you all right?" she asked, still more or less lying on top of me.

"Yeah," I said, feeling a shooting pain in my ribs. I thought I might've heard something crack when Clay landed on me, but I didn't want her jumping away just because I was hurt. "Fine," I said, getting another jab of pain as Clay shifted her weight. "How 'bout you?"

Clay said something, but I wasn't sure what. All I knew was she was still lying on top of me. Clay and I were lying together there in the snow, and I was looking up at her face about five inches away. And she was looking back at me. Clay was lying on top of me, and we were looking at each other, five inches away. Then she rested her chin on my shoulder. "Is it cold down there?"

I could feel my jeans soaking up the wet snow, but I felt warm, like everything was breaking up inside. I shook my head that it wasn't cold, and Clay and I just looked at each other. Just looked at each other without saying anything, without laughing, without smiling.

My heart started going like a psychopathic maniac because we were going to kiss! We were,

I could tell. I'd seen the movies, I knew how it happened, and I quick swallowed so my mouth wouldn't be soaking wet. Clay kept looking at me. I hated people looking at my face, but it was worth it, to kiss her, and I kept looking back at her eyes. First at one eye, then the other. Then her nose. Then her lips, which were parted slightly in a sexy way.

And then Clay climbed off me. She rolled off and sat there in the snow, her back to me. I almost asked her if she was OK, if something was wrong, but then I realized what was going on. I knew exactly what was going on, but instead of getting all hurt or mad about it, the ice came back again. She didn't want to kiss me. She got a chance to look up close, and she decided maybe not. She decided maybe friends was a better idea.

Clay kept sitting there, but I stood up, a vicious pain stabbing my ribs. I didn't want to hear any just-friends crap. I didn't want to hear how much Clay liked me—as a friend. I didn't want her being really nice and looking at me with her eyes melting with sympathy, and talking about how much she enjoys being with me. "It's just that I could never kiss you. OK? Not after looking at your face from five inches away."

I didn't feel like getting into it. And I didn't want to give her the chance to start.

"We should get going," I said, looking up at the snow, looking over at the buildings on Fifth, looking anywhere but at Clay. From the corner of my eye, I could see her slowly standing up, like she was trying to think how to say it, how to start.

"I think the temperature's dropped," I said. "I wonder what it's doing down in Washington. I forgot to check the forecast. Maybe I'll get a newspaper and check it out."

"Hale?" Very soft.

"I went through a stage when I was little where I cut the weather maps out of the newspaper every day and hung them up, side by side, in my room. I'm not sure I understood how they worked, but I loved looking at them all in a row like that. It was like I could see everything that was going on. You ready?"

I started to walk, but Clay didn't move. "You coming?" I asked, half over my shoulder, and slowly Clay took a step. And then another. I slowed down so I could stay just about a step ahead of her.

My ribs twinged when I brought my left foot down, but if I walked softly it was OK.

Once I tried to take a deep breath and had to grit my teeth to keep from screaming. Had I broken something? I was always thinking I'd broken something—ankles, toes, elbows. I wasn't about to say anything to Clay, though. All I needed was Clay finding out about the ribs and *consoling* me and saying, "Oh, by the way, did I mention I just want to be friends?"

I told her about the time I was twelve and bought a tube of theatrical blood and started screaming in the kitchen and made Tracy think I'd cut off my thumb. I was really cheerful, telling the story. I wanted it to look like I thought this whole friends idea was great so that Clay wouldn't feel guilty and wouldn't feel like she had to explain. Why is it when someone wants to be just friends, they feel like they have to *explain?* What's to explain?

The snow was piling up, so we got out of the park and crossed over to the east side of Fifth Avenue, where the doormen were busy shoveling the snow and throwing salt onto the sidewalk for all the rich people. I talked about movies and then football and then a science project in the sixth grade, where I cut open a cow's heart.

"I'm sorry," Clay said in a gap between stories.

"Did Tracy ever tell you," I said, exactly like

I hadn't heard, "how our dad sends songs he writes to Bruce Springsteen? He stopped for a while, but I think Matilda talked him into sending them again."

Clay didn't say anything.

"I used to think it was really stupid, but it's not like Dad worries about it anymore. I mean, it's not like his life depends on signing a contract with Bruce Springsteen. Dad has a pretty good attitude, actually. He wrote some lyrics of his on my birthday card:

> *'I'm learning to live with my dreams,*
> *not in them.'*

"It doesn't rhyme, but it's not bad. It's like, who cares, you know? It's no big deal. It doesn't matter. What the hell."

We got to the museum without any more apologies. Clay was quiet and actually looked mad, but I didn't care. I felt good. Even with the ribs, I felt great—icy great. It didn't matter if Clay was mad. I didn't want to hear it; I didn't care. I was ice. It didn't matter if Clay was sorry or mad or bleeding to death. I was ice. I could go on like this forever. I walked into the museum like I was listening to really loud rock and roll and nothing else mattered.

Mr. Wilson was just inside the main entrance of the museum, jumping all around with his clipboard, his hair falling down onto his forehead. A lot of kids were standing around, too, and I asked Milly Robinson what was going on. She said they were forecasting more snow, so Wilson was trying to get everyone together so we could leave early. Clay and I went over to give him our names, but as soon as he saw me, he looked like he was going to drive a stake through my heart.

"O'Reilly," he said. How'd he remember my name? "Mr. Farnsworth?" Wilson called. Farnsworth was an oversized wrestling coach with a receding hairline. "Mr. Farnsworth, you will be glad to know that *this* is Hale O'Reilly."

I looked at Clay. What was going on? Farnsworth waddled over and grabbed my arm like he was going to hang me up on the wall.

"Let's go."

I walked along with him, trying to think. "Is there something wrong?"

Farnsworth guided me toward the stairs.

"You know, I think my ribs are broken."

"I don't care if your head is broken."

Real sensitive guy, Farnsworth. He practically

233

dragged me down the stairs, which bothered my ribs a lot more than the plain walking. Then he started dragging me toward the rest rooms.

"Are you sure you've got the right guy?"

The pay phones were just outside the bathrooms, and Farnsworth threw me at one of them.

"Call your father."

"What?"

"Don't *what* me. We had to call all the parents about the snowstorm."

Oh, shit.

"Turns out your daddy doesn't know you're here, does he?"

"What. I told my stepmother."

"That's funny, because I just talked to her personally, and she didn't seem to know anything about it."

*Shit!*

"Call. Now." Farnsworth gave me a flat, thin smile. "And don't hang up, because I'll talk to them when you're through."

I took a deep breath and slowly took the receiver, trying to think. I didn't want to hear it. I wasn't in the mood for Dad yelling at me. I didn't feel like listening to him tell me about maturity and responsibility and isn't it about time I grew up. I hated that crap about growing up. I hated all of it, and I felt like screaming or kicking or shooting Farnsworth in the kneecap. I could feel my whole body overheating as I turned my back on Farnsworth and punched up the numbers.

Matilda picked up on the first ring. "Oh, thank God," she said when she heard my voice. "Oh, Hale, I'm so glad you called. Oh, I'm so glad. Are you all right? Is everything OK? Oh, Hale."

She was crying. Deep rolling sobs.

"I'm sorry."

"Oh, Haley, we were so scared. We didn't know. We were so scared. Tom said something happened last night, but he didn't know what. He and Willy went out, and all day your dad and Tracy . . . Oh, Haley, Haley." I could hear the tears. "We love you so much. We love you so much."

I was still ice. I still felt like ice but then started to say I was sorry again and felt my voice catch. I felt bad for Matilda. I couldn't believe she was crying like this. She kept telling me how glad she was and how scared they were and how sorry they were that I felt like I had to leave. I shook my head.

"No, that wasn't—" But my throat balled all up again and stuck, and I just shook my head.

I shut my eyes, not wanting to listen to any

more of Matilda crying her eyes out and saying how much they loved me. I didn't want to hear it. It was like when Mom and Dad got divorced. It was OK, everything was fine, until our neighbor Mrs. Singer started telling me how sorry she was, and all of a sudden I was bawling, tears everywhere, with my hand covering my eyes like I'd walked out of a dark room into sunlight. This phone call was the same thing. One second I was ice, and then all of a sudden, I had my eyes closed against the tears. I didn't even know what I was crying about. Matilda got me going with the we-love-you crap, and then I couldn't stop.

People were walking toward the rest rooms and looking over their shoulders at me, and I turned and tucked my head toward the phone.

" . . . oh, Haley, maybe we don't show it, but we love you so much. We really do."

"I love—" My throat closed and I nodded, not knowing what I was crying about. I didn't want it. What was going on? I rested my forehead against the top of the phone and watched the tears fall out. I wanted ice. I just wanted ice, but it wasn't there. I wasn't frozen; I couldn't shut it off. It got to me. Clay blowing me off back at the park. Sheri feeling sorry for me. Tracy looking through me. It got to me. Mom embarrassed by me; Dad and Matilda worried for me. It got to me. It just got to me.

I tried to take a deep breath, like I was finished, but it just kept coming.

"Haley, are you all right?"

I couldn't say anything.

"Haley."

"Uh-huh," I said through my teeth, still trying to stop.

"Are you OK? Is there anything I can do? Do you want me to just keep talking?"

"Uh-huh."

Matilda kept talking, and I stood there with my head on the phone, feeling like someone could pour me into a glass and drink me down like a milk shake. But it was OK. It was. It was OK. What I wanted, everything I secretly dreamed about—the good looks, the friends, the talent, the kiss—the stuff that was going to change my life—it was always going to be out there some-where. I was always going to dream it, no matter what. But in the meantime—and this right here was the meantime; I *lived* in the meantime; I might have a whole life of the meantime—in the mean-time, it was OK. I didn't have to *wait*. I didn't have to shut down, didn't have to ice people out, didn't have to sit around dreaming about what life was *going* to be like. The dreams didn't have to take over, didn't have to ruin the meantime, the now. It was OK.

*Now* was OK.

# Chapter 20

Farnsworth made sure I was the first one on the bus, and then he guarded the door. I sat in our same seat—last row, bathroom side—leaning sideways against the window so my ribs wouldn't jab me like a bunch of knitting needles. The snow had changed to a sharp rain, and the sky was a late-afternoon winter dusk. The lights were on in the bus, so I had to cup my hands across my forehead and stick my nose against the window to see outside.

Kids were standing around the bus, waiting to get on, but I didn't see Clay. She hadn't been there by the museum entrance when Farnsworth took me back upstairs, either. She had to get on the bus, though. Didn't she? I bit my lip and looked back and forth between outside and the people as they climbed up the steps into the bus. It got harder to see up front once a few people were on and kept standing around instead of sitting down like they were supposed to. I shook my head and felt like yelling something at them. I didn't want Clay sitting down up there somewhere. I wanted to talk to her. I knew she might not believe me, but I really wanted to say something to her.

There she was, walking by the driver, looking down, reading a book.

"Clay!" I called, but not loud enough. *"Clay!"* She turned to sit down in an empty seat. *"CLAY!"*

The whole bus heard that one, and maybe some people walking along the street, too. People turned around to see who the jerk was, and I waved to Clay with my right arm and pointed to the seat next to me. She just stared for a long second like she was trying to add a column of numbers in her head.

*Please?* I mouthed, and gave her my best basset-hound face. I saw Clay roll her eyes, but she walked back and free-fell into the seat next to me.

"Hi."

Clay looked at the back of the seat in front of her. "What now?"

"What. I was just saving you a seat."

Clay shut her eyes and dropped her head back against the seat. "You're too kind."

I looked at her sitting there with her eyes closed. "Actually—" I was ready to just say it, but then Clay opened her eyes and looked at me. I looked at the back of the seat in front of her. "Uh . . . I, uh . . ."

"Talk," she said.

I looked at her. "I want to be friends," I said, and looked back at the seat in front of her. "I was mad, back in the park, when you didn't want to, uh—whatever, but—I'd like to be friends." I smiled, remembering. "It was fun. I had a good time. Today."

Clay stared back at me and nodded. But then she closed her eyes and dropped her head back against the seat again. *"Hooooooooo,"* she said, emptying the air out of her lungs.

I just looked at her. "Anyway . . ." I turned toward the window. I'd said it. I was glad I'd said it. I hoped Clay didn't laugh about it with Tracy, but I was still glad I'd said it. Would she laugh about it with Tracy? She might; I wasn't sure.

They turned out the lights inside the bus and we started to roll slowly down Fifth Avenue. It was dark out now, but the snow in the park made the ground glow blue-white.

Clay reached up and pushed the button for her reading light. She bumped against me, taking off her jacket. I looked down and saw a little book on paintings that she must've bought at the museum. She grabbed the book and bumped against me again as I looked out the window at the park going by. Clay nudged my arm again, and I looked and saw her settling her head down, leaning against me like a pillow, making herself comfortable to read her book. My heart started going. This was unbelievable. Her head was resting against my arm. Just like that. Like it was no big deal, like she'd rested her head against me lots of times before, hundreds of times before.

I looked out the window. We were friends. Yeah. I wasn't going to get out of control here and start thinking all sorts of things. I'd seen girls do this all the time with their guy friends at school. I'd seen probably half the girls in the senior class lean against Willy like this. It was friendly, snuggling against someone's arm like this. Like shaking someone's hand. I just wasn't used to it because I didn't have a lot of friends who were girls. It was nice. It was great. Clay and I were friends. I liked her. She was funny, and she was nice. Most people probably didn't even know she was nice.

The bus kept going down Fifth, and I got one last quick look at the Christmas tree, which glowed bright in the closing dark.

"It's all melting," I said, looking at the little piles of snow left. I instantly regretted saying it because Clay stopped leaning against me and sat up and looked out.

"You're right. It's melting."

"Thank you."

"You're welcome," Clay said, and nestled right back down against my arm and kept reading her book. "Did Tracy tell you it was your fault she and me and Mickey and everyone got arrested at the football game?"

"What?"

"We were out in the parking lot. While I was telling them what a pig you were, I made some really gross pig sounds and everyone laughed. So I didn't stop. I kept snorting away as loud as I could, and a cop walking by thought I was making fun of him."

"That's really true? You guys really got arrested for making pig sounds?"

"No. We got arrested because you were a

pig," Clay said, nestling some more to try to get comfortable. "And I promised myself I would never give you the chance to make me look stupid ever again."

When did I make her look stupid? I didn't know. All I knew was that Clay was grabbing my hand—I watched, like it was a movie, like it was someone else. Clay grabbed my hand, lifted my arm, draped it over herself, and leaned her head in to snuggle against my side.

I squeezed my eyes closed tight, seeing stars and understanding how people could faint from pain. This was awful. It was wonderful but awful. She could've been stabbing me. She could've been digging between my ribs with her bare hand and pulling something out.

The pain died down pretty fast, though, once Clay settled in. It stopped feeling like internal damage was going on, and I tried to breathe again with my other lung. My hand was resting on Clay's hip. Right there on the side of her hip. Did friends do this? I knew they snuggled. I knew they were always putting their arms around each other. It always kind of surprised me, actually, what friends did, how they touched each other. They probably rested hands on each other's hips; who knows?

For me, it was something new and wonderful, though.

Clay moved a little to turn a page, sticking another knife into my side. I had to say something. I was going to have to say something, eventually. What if there was internal bleeding? What if I was sitting here dying and didn't know it?

Maybe I felt like I was running out of time, or maybe I was just stupid, but, without thinking about it, I moved my hand from Clay's hip and gently touched her arm. I brushed my fingers along her upper arm, back and forth. She was wearing a long-sleeved shirt, but I could feel the warmth through the material. Did friends do this? Was it something friends could do? I kept looking at the window, every second waiting for Clay to say "Stop." The bus shot into the Lincoln Tunnel and then out into the black night of Jersey. Once I took a quick look at the hand over there, caressing Clay's arm. It was my hand. It was connected to my wrist.

Clay shifted herself—more pain, a lot of it. I pictured a rib poking into a pink lung. My eyes shut tight and my toes curled, and I was about to say something, when Clay reached up and grabbed the hand I had on her arm and pulled it down under her chin and held on to it. Our hands were hooked together there under Clay's chin. This wasn't friends. Was it? Was this friends? Snuggled together, holding hands on a bus at night, speeding down the Jersey Turnpike. Was that friends? Maybe. Maybe it was friends. I didn't know. I looked out the window and felt my hand in Clay's. I pressed her fingers, and she pressed back. She knew we were holding hands. She didn't act like it wasn't happening.

I pressed her hand again, and Clay brought my hand up to her mouth and kissed my knuckle. First with a little kiss, then with a longer open-mouth kiss where she gently bit my knuckle.

Not friends, this. Oh, God. No, not friends. No. My heart was going up in flames. This was better than what I imagined *sex* would be like, almost. She liked me. Clay liked me. I liked Clay and Clay liked me. I'd always imagined something like this, but it was a lot better when it was real.

"Clay?" I said, almost laughing because I could say it now; I didn't mind saying it—it was OK; it was OK to say it. It wouldn't ruin everything. She liked me. I could say it. "Clay?"

"Mmm?"

"I think my ribs are broken."